The Woods are Watching

NARENDRA JAILALL

This is a work of fiction. Names, characters and incidents are either the products of the author's imagination or used in a fictitious manner. Any resemblance to actual persons, living or dead, or actual events is purely coincidental.

To contact author: njailall@hotmail.com

ISBN: 978-1-989403-22-8

Edited by: Sabi Jailall

Design & Layout: ThePublishingMentor.com

Published through: In Our Words Inc.

Contents

Dedication

This book is dedicated to the teachers and students of
Derry West Village Public School,
Ruth Thompson Middle School
and Ingleborough Public School.

Your spirit, inspiration and genuineness
helped make this story possible.

Chapter 1

Spring Meadow and Beyond

I'd tell you my name, but it's not important.

Nothing is important when you have moved to a new neighbourhood and school. You're just "the new kid," the one who looks around at the strange walls and doors, the one who is being told how many periods are scheduled in a day and the dismissal times. All of this while you are trying to memorize the location of the nearest washroom and water fountain.

Mrs. Macmillan was more like my tour guide than the first teacher I met at Spring Meadow Middle School. She was a plump, dark-haired woman with glasses who acted a little too excited and jolly for her own good. She and I moved down the hallways and endless rows of lockers.

"Oh, you will just love it here at Spring Meadow!" she told me. "The staff and students are great because we all have that 'spring' in our step!" She chuckled at her own joke. "You'll see. Everything will be just peachy!"

Peachy? I thought. *More like a sour lemon.* I wondered if she had ever moved to a new school with no friends trying to get used to a new way of doing things.

We arrived at Room 207. The door was already open and right away I felt twenty-six pairs of eyes on me. The teacher strode from his desk and came over to Mrs. Macmillan and me.

She handed him some forms, said a few words then left.

I found out that this teacher's name was Mr. Stellick. He was my homeroom teacher. He seemed okay but the challenge would be surviving this Grade 7 world of wild boys and mini-teen girls who looked at you more than they needed to.

As I sat by the desk near the window I could feel the cool April air on my arms but the hot stares of the students wondering who this new girl was made me self-conscious. I tried concentrating on what Mr. Stellick was saying but was too nervous knowing I was being watched.

It got a little easier as each period went by that morning. Students seemed to be getting used to me even though they didn't say much. The hallway shook with loud voices, moving bodies, swinging binders and gym bags as people made their way to the lunchroom or the closest exit. I got closer to my locker and panicked for a moment when I saw that it was wide open. The locker door swung shut and standing right in front of it was a short girl with black hair.

"Hi," she greeted.

"Hi," I replied nervously.

"I'm Linh, your locker partner." She extended her hand.

I shook it lightly. "My name's Dhanika. I'm new here."

"Yeah, I know," Linh said. "I had this locker to myself for a while ever since Jayden moved."

"Who is Jayden?"

"My friend who used to go here. She'll probably be back sometime next year when we're in Grade 8. She's always moving then coming back then moving..." Linh waved her hand back and forth.

"Kind of like a yo-yo?" I offered.

"Yeah!" Linh smiled. "Or a boomerang." She turned the dial on the combination lock, gave it a tug and pulled the door open.

"I don't have much stuff," she told me. "The top shelf

is all yours and you can use the very bottom if you need it. I just use the second shelf and this mirror." Linh pointed to a pink plastic framed rectangle on the inside door. "Good for checking if your face is Zit City! Not that yours is or anything."

I laughed. "Thanks."

"You've got the lock combination, right?" Linh asked.

"Yeah. The secretary gave it to me this morning."

"Okay." Linh paused and looked me up and down. "You seem nice, unlike some of the other girls around here. I have to go now but I'll see you later!"

Just then, I got a warm feeling throughout my whole body. It wasn't one of those feelings you get when your body overheats with a fever. It was more like being under a soft, thick blanket in your bed as the cold rain and wind rap the window on a dark night. Linh had just given me a big hug without even touching me. She turned and walked down the hall.

Would she be my first friend?

Our new house is in a small suburban city named Sterling Creek. Actually, I shouldn't say it's small. There are close to one million people living here. It is pretty ordinary to tell you the truth. Most of the houses are new and all of the lawns have a rich green colour. There are a couple of shopping malls, a bunch of cookie-cutter plazas with grocery stores, convenience stores, nail salons and places that serve burgers and wings. When you look around at the stores, houses and cars, everything is pretty much the same. It probably looks a lot like your community.

The neighbourhood is mostly quiet, except when the little kids run around and play loudly outside on their lawns and sidewalks. There are a few girls and boys my age on this street. Sometimes they rollerblade or ride their bikes trying to look cooler than they actually are. I think they go to my school but I haven't seen them there yet.

My family is just my dad and me. My mom left when I

was four years old. We used to live in a town called Stansford, just outside of the city. Sadly, the only thing I remember from when I was little is seeing and hearing the arguing and fighting between her and dad. I used to lie in bed and push the openings of my ears tightly with my middle fingers but even that didn't drown out their angry voices and shouting. Mom was always upset at dad over his work. His official title is 'software developer' but I don't really know a lot about his job. I just know that he works long hours. Mom thought if he put more time and effort into his family instead of trying to come up with the next big invention he'd be a better father and husband. Dad used to tell her to stop being pushy and angry all the time. He tried to assure mom that things would get better at home when things at work got better and he got promoted.

This was one of many things on which they disagreed and finally mom couldn't take it and left. She lives about twenty minutes away in Hammondville and for a while I used to see her about four or five times a month. Over the last few years we lost touch. I tried phoning but never heard from her. Maybe she took an extended vacation.

You might be wondering why I ended up living with my dad. He is actually very nice and doesn't get upset as quickly as mom did. It makes me wonder sometimes how they ever got married in the first place. Dad gives me as much space as I want but still takes the time to talk to me in the evenings or sometimes in the morning before he heads off to work. He is usually home on the weekends and we do things together on those days. We go for walks, drives or to the movie theatre. Dad is also a good cook. We fool around in the kitchen inventing all kinds of new things. One of my favourites is baked macaroni balls with jalapeños and ketchup. Mom was never that creative with food. Cooking was one of many things she took too seriously.

Even though mom wasn't as fun as dad, I still miss her.

I get sad sometimes when I see mothers with their sons and daughters at the park or mall talking and playing or just being angry at each other. The angry moments don't last forever. They go away sooner or later. But the emptiness of not having a mother is always around. I try not to think about it but it's hard.

To sort of make up for not having a mom around, dad hired a nanny last year. Her name is Jocelyn and she's from the Philippines. Sometimes I call her "Joss" for short. I never understood how Jocelyn could have the title 'nanny.' To me, a nanny is a woman in a rocking chair with grey hair and glasses that are tilted far down her nose. These nannies give you graham crackers and milk and remind you to eat all your vegetables as they tell you how much things have changed. They always end their sentences with, "They don't make 'em like they used to..." Jocelyn is the opposite—young, pretty and in her early 20s, with no rocking chair. She stays with us during the week when dad works late and is always around when I get home from school in the afternoon.

Our new neighbourhood might be bland in ways but one thing I really like about it is Sterling Creek Community Centre. It's this massive building with a swimming pool, library, art studios, gymnasium, indoor skating rink and meeting rooms. There is so much to do there and that's just the inside. Outside, you will find a large park, tennis courts, soccer field, baseball diamonds and bike paths. The bike paths take you around the entire community centre and down a trail to a huge, thick forest only a few hundred feet away. Sterling Creek runs through this forest which has so much wildlife. This is a big deal for me because I love animals. The forest stretches for miles and is one place that's untouched by houses and stores. It is a place that holds so much wonderment and adventure, I cannot even begin to write down or tell you how exciting it looks from the outside.

But I found out later on that it is also the place the neighbourhood children were told never to enter, especially when it got dark. We were told bad things would happen if we ever did.

Chapter 2

Tales from Sterling Creek

I don't know why the grown-ups in Sterling Creek made the children afraid of the forest. Maybe they were scared we would get lost or attacked by some wild animals. To me, being surrounded by trees, flowers and wildlife was an escape from stuff I didn't like and people who were sometimes mean and unfair.

I understood why parents wanted to protect us and keep us safe but only allowing us to play on driveways and sidewalks meant we were missing out on all of the neat and exciting things you could find among trees and bushes. So why keep us away from nature? I don't know about you but I would rather fall down on a forest floor than on a hard driveway.

To keep intruders out, a large fence was erected around the entire forest. Large, white, metal signs were fastened to the fence that read 'NO TRESPASSING BY ORDER OF THE CITY OF STERLING CREEK AND THE POLICE DEPARTMENT.' Police officers in cruisers or on foot would patrol areas around the forest a few times a week but the fence and especially the scary stories were more than enough to keep us away.

Whatever the adults told the children about the forest before I moved to Sterling Creek seemed to have worked. I found out that kids used the community centre and bike paths but never really broke the no trespassing rule. Some teenagers would hang around the perimeter but never went too far inside the forest.

We were told stories of boys and girls who were said to have disappeared. The local police and members of city council explored the forest and said they heard strange noises—noises that didn't sound like animals. They warned of evil spirits in and around the trees, probably they said of people from Sterling Creek who had died a long time ago. And the more these tales were told, the more believable they became. The haunted, dangerous forest was as real as the sky is blue. That's how it is. If people keep saying something is true, it eventually becomes a 'fact' and everyone just accepts it.

Some of us wondered if the forest was really haunted even though we were warned and scared into believing what was inside. You know how it is—parents tell their kids not to do something but we just have to find out for ourselves. We're curious that way. I guess with us, if it feels right, we just go ahead and do it even though it frustrates our parents and sometimes makes them angry. Does this sound familiar?

Parent: "Put on your hat and gloves. It's cold outside."

You: "But mom, it's April!"

Parent: "So what? They're for your own protection. Do you know how much hats and gloves cost when I was your age? Back then, we'd have to walk fifty kilometres to school. And that was one way! Then we'd have chores to do, homework, water to be carried from the river in a pail which had a hole at the bottom..."

You would let them talk about when they were kids and of course at the end you would leave home with your jacket on but unzip or take it off the first chance you got.

One day at lunch, Linh told me about two seventeen-year-olds named Kyle Everill and Sameer Chokshi who wanted to see things for themselves. They refused to accept those 'forest facts' and thought that the stories were ridiculous. Kyle's dad works at city hall and was one of those adults who went into the forest and warned everyone about it afterward. You would have thought his own son would have been scared the most but he wasn't. Kyle and Sameer decided to sneak out one night and check it out. Forget about playing outside in April without your jacket against your parents' rules. This was much bigger than that.

I was told they met at the trail behind the community centre and entered the forest. There was a cool breeze that night and Kyle and Sameer walked for about ten minutes among the trees. They weren't sure where they were going since there were no dirt or paved paths so they just shone their flashlights and tried to get a good look around.

I was just going to say that what they saw was 'spooky' but that isn't even the right word for it. 'Spooky' is just a word that little boys and girls use around Halloween to describe their cute costumes or a house with no lights on. Every street has a house like this. In my old neighbourhood, everyone knew that Ms. Edwards lived in the house on the corner lot and never gave out candy to trick-or-treaters. So I would just skip her house. And it wasn't as if we didn't know her. We would see her during the day working in the front garden or on weekends taking groceries into her house.

What Sameer and Kyle saw, or think they saw that night, was straight up *frightening*. The night wind caused the branches and bushes to shake so it looked as though something was waiting ready to jump out and attack. Kyle recalled some of the branches having torn bits of denim shirts and strange wooden stakes in the ground the shape of crosses. The tall trees were twisted and their bark had knots that looked like the faces of demons and gargoyles.

Sameer said these movements, crosses and faces were

only the beginning. The most terrifying part about being in a forest late at night was the noise. You had no idea from where it was coming but it was the most disturbing and evil sound you ever heard. They remembered hearing a low, gurgling sound that seemed to be all around them, like some kind of creature with cold, heavy breathing. In the distance there were hissing and groans of pain. The two friends turned to go back but were tackled to the ground by something and ended up passing out. They woke up in hospital beds but aside from a few bruises and scratches, were okay. Since then, nobody, especially children, has gone into Sterling Creek Forest.

School had gotten better over the last month. I met a few students in my classes who were friendly. Sarah, a tall girl in my math class and Prathanan, a medium-built boy with a short haircut who sat at my table group in French. They were both easy to talk to. But, just like in every school, there are some unkind moments. They happen so quickly, yet are powerful enough to ruin someone's entire day.

I walked down the hall after geography one morning and passed a few girls standing by a locker. One was checking her hair in a mirror and the other two stood on either side. I looked at the two of them and kept going.

"Loser," one said. The group giggled.

I turned around. "What did you say?"

"Nothing," she replied. "You must be hearing things." She flicked a strand of brown hair streaked with blonde away from her eye.

The other girl spoke, trying to defend her. "Uh, my friend sneezed, okay?"

I felt my body heating up. "It's called a tissue. Try using one sometime."

"Whatever," the first one said.

I shook my head and walked away. The girls gathered around the little mirror, posing and cackling, wondering who was the fairest of them all. I arrived at my locker. Linh was there. Immediately she knew something was wrong.

"Hi," she said. "You okay?"

"Yeah. Just a few stupid girls." I told her what happened.

Linh nodded. "I know who they are. They think they're better than everyone else because they have nice clothes and stuff."

"I tried not to show that they got to me but it's tough," I admitted. "Why do they have to be so mean? They don't even know me!"

Linh was quiet. "I don't know."

The silence continued. Then Linh spoke again.

"Let's walk home after school. You ever had a D.D.C.?"

"No. What's that?"

"Dan's Double Chocolate Cone. You'll love it!"

I smiled. "Sure."

That afternoon, Linh and I walked across the park and three blocks later arrived at Ridgemount Plaza. We entered the convenience store. A bell jingled as the door closed behind us. Linh led me over to the freezer with a sliding glass cover. She took out two D.D.Cs and headed over to the cashier's counter. Soon we were on the sidewalk again biting into our treats.

"Mmm," I remarked. "This is really good!"

"Yeah," said Linh. "Wait 'till you get to the chocolate cone. That's the best part."

She was right. The rippled cone had a soft strip of chocolate on the inside that I hardly needed to chew. It just melted in my mouth.

"That was awesome. Thanks!" I told her. I was feeling better now.

"I thought you'd like it," Linh replied.

We passed some houses and got to a four-way intersection. A crossing guard walked with us, then we continued along the sidewalk.

"You have a lot of homework?" Linh asked.

"Not too much, if you mean textbook questions," I said. "I have a project and a test coming up."

"Think you'll be finished by next weekend?" she asked.

"I guess." I looked at her. "Why?"

"I'm having a sleepover and was hoping you could come," Linh said.

I became excited. "Wow! Cool. That's a great idea!"

"It'll be next Friday at 6:00. I'm inviting two other girls from our school. No one to worry about. I think you'll like them."

"Okay. I'll ask my dad tonight. I think he'll be okay with it."

"We'll watch a movie, listen to some tunes and have some pizza," Linh said. "And you don't need to bring a sleeping bag. There's so many air mattresses in my house, it's like a bouncy castle!"

I laughed. "I can't wait!"

Linh's block was coming up on the left. Mine was a few minutes away. "There's something else I wanted to ask you," she said.

"What's that?"

"Do you believe in ghosts?"

Chapter 3

Maging Malakas

I was puzzled. "That's weird."

"What?" asked Linh. "Ghosts?"

"No. The question. Why? Is your house haunted or something?" I asked, smiling.

Linh laughed. "No, no. I'm just asking."

"I don't believe in them," I told her. "Do you?"

"Yeah."

"Why?"

She shrugged. "I don't know. When weird stuff happens around here, I feel like it's ghosts or spirits or something."

"You mean that scary stuff in the forest?"

"Yeah. Plus some other things I hear at night. Strange, creaky noises when everyone's asleep."

I thought for a moment. There were noises I used to hear at night and sometimes during the day. In a way, it was kind of annoying. My house in this new neighbourhood is only two years old! There shouldn't be anything wrong with it. I could never figure out what made the noises or where they came from.

Still, did that mean a ghost or some other freaky thing was causing them? Maybe it was bats or mice in the attic. I didn't know. And not knowing was probably the worst part.

Having no idea how a problem started and if or when it would ever end.

I decided to lighten the mood.

"Maybe you're behind the noises. Do you snore?" We both laughed.

I continued. "I don't believe stuff until I see it. I haven't seen ghosts or anything close to them and until I do, they're just made up." I spoke these words bravely, believing only some of them.

"But what if they are real and we just haven't seen them yet? And one night when you get up to go to the bathroom, you turn the corner and BOO! They leap out and scare you out of your PJs!" Linh said.

I smiled a little but underneath, worry began to stick tiny pins inside my stomach. Suddenly, the sleepover did not seem like the best idea. Linh must have sensed my nervousness.

"The house is fine," she reassured. "I haven't seen anything strange or weird lately. Except when my older sister's getting ready in front of the mirror. Trust me, those dance moves could send the scariest ghosts back to their graves!"

I laughed and felt a little better. Then Linh turned towards her block. "I better get going," she said.

"Okay. Thanks for the D.D.C.!"

"No problem. See ya!"

As I walked home, I could not help thinking why Linh would ask me about ghosts. It's a weird question that is a little creepy but at the same time fun to wonder about. But wasn't it strange that she had mentioned ghosts right after inviting me to a sleepover? Why tell someone something nice and then say a bad thing afterward? It's like telling your friend, 'I heard you got a new bike. That's so cool! But aren't you scared you're going to fall off it and break your neck?'

When I got home, I made up my mind to go to the sleepover. I figured nothing bad would happen and Linh did say that the two other girls weren't anyone to worry about. I was looking forward to making some new friends.

I went upstairs and changed into an old t-shirt and track pants. I shuffled down the steps and headed into the kitchen. Joss was standing by the sink and greeted me.

"How was your day?"

"Fine." I opened the fridge door and poured myself a glass of apple juice.

"Do you want something to eat?" she offered. "A sandwich? Pizza pocket?"

"No, I'm okay, thanks."

I took a swig of juice and tapped a pattern on the table as I stared straight ahead. The thin trees swayed outside the kitchen window as they showed off their buds. Soon, sprouting leaves and final report cards would mark the arrival of summer.

"Dinner's on the stove," Joss said. "Have it whenever you're ready."

"Thanks. I'll wait for dad. There's something I want to ask him."

"Anything I can help you with?" offered Joss.

"No. I'm going to ask him if I can go to my friend's sleepover next Friday."

"Oh. Sounds like fun. Who's your friend?"

"A girl... my friend. You don't know her. Anyway, I think it'll be good but I'm kind of worried about it."

Joss sat down across from me. "What's bothering you?"

I told her about the ghost discussion Linh and I had on our walk home. Joss nodded silently. Then she spoke.

"Back in the Philippines, when I was your age, I used to sleepover at my cousins' house..."

Here we go, I thought. I got my poor ears ready to listen to a grown-up's story about sleepovers and what they did for fun in the olden days of the 1970s or whatever ancient decade they were a kid. Same old, boring stuff but I listened anyway.

"Connie, our oldest cousin, used to tell us scary stories about a demon that would hide in corners of the house. She'd take us to different parts of the house late at night and show us the places where the demon lay. And we'd all see its claws and evil eye staring at us. This used to frighten us so much, we couldn't go to sleep. Then one sleepover, three of us cousins had had enough. Joramae, Grace and I decided to find out what the scary thing was all about. Turned out it was just plants that my aunt had in the corners of her house!"

"What? That's it?" I asked. "No demon or monster?"

Joss laughed. "No! The 'claws' were the hanging plant leaves and the 'evil eyes' were the yellow and red flower parts! The light from the windows made them look scary."

I felt relieved. "That's good to know."

"The world looks like a different place at night," she reminded me. "But it's nothing to be scared of. '*Maging malakas. Huwag mong kalimutan ang iyong kaibigan.*'"

"What's that?" I asked.

"Tagalog—my language. It means 'Be brave and remember your friends.' If they're true friends, they'll help you."

I went upstairs and finished my fractions homework. When nothing on TV held my interest, I went on my dad's computer in the study and played a few games. Around 7:30, I heard him open the front door and ascend the stairs.

"Hey Dhanny," he greeted me from the study entrance. Then walked over to me.

I looked up from my game. "Hi."

"Everything okay?" He sounded tired as he gently touched my head.

"Yeah."

"Good. Did you eat yet?"

"No, let's go downstairs," I said.

As I followed him down, I couldn't help noticing that his

pace was a bit slower lately. He is in his mid-thirties so he's not really old but these days dad seemed a little heavier and worn out.

We sat down and ate the noodles with mushrooms and chicken that Joss had made for us. Between bites and sips, dad told me about something he was working on that had an expanded memory and could store computer files and stuff. I nodded and said very little.

"What's new with you? School's been okay?"

"Yeah, it's been good. I got invited to a sleepover next Friday night. Can I go?"

Dad was silent. "Whose sleepover?"

"My locker partner, Linh."

He had a serious look as he shook his head. "No."

"What!? Why not?"

"Because, who's going to be around to try out my new chicken wing recipe?" He smiled.

"Come on, dad! You're kidding, right?"

"About the wings? No. The sleepover? Yes. Go ahead. You'll be back Saturday afternoon, right?"

"Yeah. There'll be enough time to make those wings. I'll even help you."

"Help me make them or eat them?" he joked.

"Both!" We laughed.

"Just get me Linh's parents' number. I want to talk to them first and give them a number where I can be reached."

"Thanks, dad!" I bolted from my chair and hugged him around the neck.

He patted my hand and looked at me. "I'm glad you made a friend."

"Yeah. And there'll be a couple of other girls from my classes there!"

"Oh boy," he said. "Four girls under one roof? Try to put the 'sleep' in 'sleepover' when you're there!"

I rolled my eyes and began to clear the table. Joss came and took over the clean up.

That night I fell asleep peacefully but woke up several hours later and needed to go to the bathroom. I started to feel afraid, until I remembered Joss's words about the night. There was nothing to be afraid of, right? I bravely got out of bed and dashed across the hall. My head moved left to right, looking and listening. Actually all of my senses were on full alert, ready to detect any strange noises. I heard nothing and felt relaxed after I was finished in the bathroom.

As I made my way back, I turned on the lamp in the hallway to guide me back to my room. And just before I climbed into bed, I switched on my nightlight, just in case. It might be for babies but so what? I wasn't going to take any chances.

Chapter 4

Truth or Dare

The first things I noticed about Linh's house when I arrived a few minutes after six Friday evening were the plants at the front. Her family seemed to spend a lot of time cleaning and watering. The flowers were not in full bloom yet but I could tell they would be a pretty set of colours when the time was right. The neatly-trimmed bushes along the front and sides made the house look like the ones you see on TV or in books. It was very colourful compared to the front of my house that just had grass and a boring concrete walkway that led to the front door.

I rang the doorbell and in a few seconds Mrs. Tran appeared.

"Hi Dhanika!" she greeted. "Nice to finally meet you." She waved at dad. He waved back, honked the car horn and pulled off.

"Hi," I replied. "Nice to meet you too."

"Linh will be up in a minute. Sarah and Zoe are already here. Linh! Your friend is here!" Mrs. Tran called.

The inside of the house was just as pretty as the outside. Antiques and decorations were displayed on shelves or rested on the shiny, unscratched floor and framed family pictures could be seen on the walls of the hallway and other rooms. I noticed the children seemed happiest. The old people, probably the grandparents, didn't smile. They looked like someone had taken their picture when they were changing a baby's diaper. I hid my smile carefully so that Mrs. Tran wouldn't notice and ask me what was so funny. The scent of the house entering my nostrils was pleasant. It was a combination of lemon and pine but not enough to make me sneeze.

I heard the basement door open and Linh rushed towards me. "Hey! How's it going?" She gave me a little hug.

"Great!" I replied. "This is so exciting!"

"Have fun girls. We'll be upstairs if you need anything," reminded Mrs. Tran.

"Okay. Thanks, mom!" Linh said.

I followed Linh down the steps into the basement. Its walls were white and the ground was half floor and half carpet. The TV in the corner was on the weather channel for some reason and there was a kitchen off to the side as well as a few doors that led somewhere. I put my backpack down beside the couch. Sarah and another girl were sitting on the floor nibbling on some chips and veggies with dip. Sarah looked up and brushed her brown bangs from her eyes.

"Hi," I greeted.

"Hey!" replied Sarah. "How's it going?"

"Pretty good." I looked at the other girl but could barely remember seeing her in the halls or rooms at Spring Meadow. Her hair was dark and short and she wore thick-rimmed glasses.

I extended my hand. "Hi. I'm Dhanika."

She shook it and gave me an odd look raising her eyebrows. "Hi. Zoe," she replied flatly, almost as if she were asking me her name.

This one's a bit of a weirdo but whatever, I thought to myself. *I'll give her a chance.*

Linh pulled me over to the table. "Have a snack," she instructed. "Something to keep you going 'til we order the pizza."

"Thanks," I said, helping myself to some chips and veggie sticks dipped in ranch dressing. I then poured about half a cup of orange pop and headed back to the couches to join everyone.

"Okay. I have a bunch of stuff planned for us but what do you all want to do first?" Linh asked.

"What kind of stuff?" asked Sarah.

"Some board games like Round the Globe and Four in a Row. And there's a deck of cards and a movie."

I spoke up. "Oh yeah? What movie?"

"Mansion of Doom!" said Linh, disguising her voice to sound scary. "Any of you seen it?"

We all shook our heads.

"I haven't either but it's supposed to be really creepy!" Everyone giggled.

After I changed into my pyjamas, we played some different card games. Sometimes we played individually and other times we played in pairs. The deluxe pizza that was ordered arrived after 8:00. We enjoyed a few slices and dunked some of our crusts in the dipping sauce, pretending we were artists about to create the world's greatest pizza painting. I felt happy, relaxed and full. I was almost going to say that I was ready to go to sleep but there was more to come on this special night.

"What do you want to do now?" Linh asked.

I shrugged. "It's your party. I like everything so far. You decide."

"Put on Mansion of Doom," Sarah suggested. "And we'll see who gets freaked out and wets themselves first!" We all laughed, until Linh stopped us.

"No, no, no. New rule! New rule! Anyone who wets anything, cleans it!" We all burst out laughing again.

"How about 'Truth or Dare?'" suggested Zoe.

Linh, Sarah and I looked at each other, then at Zoe. "What?"

"You mean, you've never heard of it?" asked Zoe, in a way that made us feel like the dumbest girls in the world.

"Yeah, I've heard of it but why do you want to play that?" asked Sarah.

"It's fun and you get to know who your friends really are," Zoe replied. "We all dare each other to say or do stuff." She smiled, showing a few crooked teeth.

This girl was strange and annoying. Why did Linh think she could be my friend? *I dare you to visit a dentist tomorrow,* I thought to myself.

"I don't know," I said. "What if we don't want to say stuff about ourselves?"

"Then you have to do a dare. Something funny or weird... anything, really," Zoe told us.

Linh wasn't sure about Zoe's suggestion either. "What if we get mad or make fun of someone," she asked. "Everything's been great so far. Why ruin it?"

Zoe brushed away at some wrinkles on her pyjama bottom. "Let's just try it. If it's no fun, we'll stop." Sarah, Linh and I agreed with some nervousness and we did rock, paper, scissors to see who'd go first. Linh won and the game began.

"Okay," Linh said. "I dare Sarah to shove six crackers in her mouth and whistle."

"No, no," interrupted Zoe. "Start like this: 'Truth, dare, double dare, promise to repeat.'"

"Wait, wait," I said. "What's this 'double dare' stuff?"

"Double dares are when you dare people to do stuff that's extra weird or crazy. Like a dare times two," Zoe pointed out.

"Truth, dare, double dare, promise to repeat," said Linh to Sarah.

"Dare," Sarah told her.

"Do the cracker thing I just told you," instructed Linh.

We all had a good laugh as Sarah whistled and blew cracker crumbs on the carpet.

The game continued with each of us having to repeat silly rhymes and words or eat a pizza crust or chip that had fallen on the floor. Some of it was funny but most of it was nonsense and kind of a waste of time. I didn't feel I knew Sarah or Zoe any more or less than before Truth or Dare had started. It was Zoe's turn. She gave me one of her weird looks as I accepted a double dare. I squeezed my left hand in a fist wondering what on earth she would make me do.

"I double dare you to go into Sterling Creek Forest," Zoe told me.

I was a bit startled and looked at her with some confusion. "What? Right now, in my pyjamas?"

"Yeah. Why not?" she asked, with her crazy eyes widening.

"Because my mom will find out and kill us, that's why," Linh interjected. "We wouldn't make it through the front door!"

"What about that door over there?" asked Zoe, pointing to the corner. "That leads outside, doesn't it?"

It felt as though some wrinkly, clammy hands were tightening their grip around my neck. I tried to make the feeling disappear by clearing my throat.

"Yes, but nobody's going out tonight, unless they sleepwalk or something!" Linh said. I felt a little better when she said that.

"And since when did Truth or Dare become an outdoor game?" asked Sarah.

Zoe put her arms up in surrender. "Okay, okay," she told us. "Just trying to have a little fun."

"Think of something else," Sarah told her.

Zoe thought for a moment and then turned to me. "Truth?" she asked.

I nodded.

"What's the most precious thing you have?"

Should I share it with them now? I wondered. I thought for a moment. *Sure. Why not?*

I reached down the neckline of my T-shirt where the imaginary, clammy hands were and pulled it out. It was a pendant hooked to a gold chain. I held the pendant up for everyone to see. It gleamed under the basement lights.

"Cool," said Sarah. "That's really pretty."

"Thanks," I said.

"Where'd you get it?" asked Linh.

"My mom gave it to me. It has two parts. Mine says 'THER D HTER.'"

"What's that?" asked Zoe.

"It spells out 'mother and daughter,'" I told her. "My mom has the other half."

"Did your mom go somewhere?" asked Sarah.

"Yeah, she lives in Hammondville. My parents are separated," I told them even though Linh already knew.

"Oh," said Zoe.

"I wear this to keep my mom close to me," I said, returning the chain and pendant back under my T-shirt. After a bit of a struggle I think I was able to re-hook it.

We were quiet for a moment. Then Linh spoke up.

"Let's do something else," Linh suggested. "How about Mansion of Doom?"

"Sure!" We all agreed but were growing sleepy. We managed to watch about half the movie without wetting anything but found ourselves nodding off. Each of us climbed on to our air mattress, covered up and then Linh turned off the lights. Within minutes we were asleep.

I don't know how long I had been asleep but was awakened by a bright flash. At first, I thought we left the TV on. Or maybe I was dreaming about something from Mansion of Doom but then I heard a loud thunderclap and knew that my biggest fear was happening in a strange house.

I shut my eyes tightly, hoping the thunderstorm would be over soon. When it didn't stop, I jerked my head to the other side of my pillow. For some reason my neck felt lighter. I touched it with my hand and a shock passed through my body.

My chain and pendant were gone!

Through the basement windows, the spidery lightning brightened the room enough for me to look around quickly. Linh and Sarah were sleeping peacefully on their sides. Then I saw Zoe's bed.

It was empty.

Chapter 5

Where the Path Leads

I sat up on the air mattress. My eyes darted across the room looking for any sign of Zoe. I scanned the corners and doors, hoping to see a tiny strip of light which would show that the washroom was being used. Nothing. Only darkness and black shadows. I then moved my hands around the pillows and sheets, in search of my pendant and chain. My hand touched a wet spot of drool. I immediately turned over the pillow. Next sleepover I'll need to pack a bib.

I decided not to wake the others and search for Zoe on my own. If I couldn't find her in the next few minutes I would ask Linh for help. I swung my legs to the right and sprang up from the soft carpet. There was no flashlight to use so I walked over to the wall and tried flicking the light switch. The basement remained dark. *Blackout*, I thought. I'd have to use the lightning's brightness that flashed across the room every minute or two.

The next bit of lightning showed me one of the doors on the far-left side was ajar. Come to think of it, I remembered hearing the wind whistling as though it were inside the house. I nervously walked over to the door.

Droplets of rain landed on my face and I could feel small, wet blobs under my feet that had entered Linh's basement uninvited. Suddenly, I realized that this was no storage room or garage. There was a concrete path in front of me and bushes on either side. I was one step away from being outside and maybe not too far from Zoe. But where would this path take me? And should I do this alone? I was worried but decided to go out for a minute and if I spotted anything weird or scary would run back and get Linh. How else would I stop being afraid, right?

The path was wet and cold but I took slow, cautious steps. I kept walking forward but always inched back a bit ready to scream and run back to the open basement door if anything creepy freaked me out. My heart thumped but I kept going, looking left to right. I could make out the bricks at the side of the house as well as some thick bushes.

Then just a few feet ahead, there was a bench. Maybe not the bench you're thinking of—the kind people sit on while waiting for a bus. I could tell that this was a fancy park bench with handles on the side. The tinny sound the rain made when it hit it told me that it was mostly metal. Almost all of it was covered by some overhanging leaves and branches. And sitting underneath that part with her back to me was Zoe.

Did she sleepwalk? *I don't want to startle her,* I thought, *but forget about scaring her! What if I go up to her, touch her on the shoulder and some demon child turns around with reptilian eyes and vampire teeth like the ones in the movies? I'd be a scaredy cat for life!*

I played it safe and kept my distance. "Zoe!" I called.

She slowly turned around. No reptile eyes, that's good, I thought. "Hello," she said in a pleasant voice. You would have thought we were having a nice talk on a picnic blanket on a sunny afternoon.

"What are you doing out here? Come back inside!" I told her.

"Thinking and facing one of my fears," she replied.

"What?" I asked.

"You asked me what I'm doing and I told you."

"Can't you do that inside where it's dry?"

"Yes but that wouldn't be any fun, would it?" she asked smiling, showing those misshapen teeth.

I felt a little better knowing that I wasn't the only one who was scared of thunderstorms. But to come out in the middle of the night to practise being brave in the middle of one? That's nuts!

Zoe held up something that looked mostly stringy. "Anyone missing a pendant?" she asked.

My pendant! I was so happy it wasn't gone forever and was about to thank her, when I remembered where I was—the side of my friend's house with a weird girl who thought there was nothing wrong with wandering outside in the middle of the night acting like Mother Nature's daughter.

"What are you doing with that?" I asked her angrily.

"Protecting it."

"From what?"

"It was lying on the floor near your bed. I spotted it just before I came out here." I walked over to her and held my hand out. She dropped it into my palm.

"If that's so precious to you, you should take better care of it," Zoe said, giving me one of her strange, fishy looks through her glasses.

"I would've found it if you just left it near my bed!"

"Maybe you would have, maybe you wouldn't."

I wiped some water from my forehead. "I'm going inside. If you want to have a sleepover with the rain and wind that's your business." I turned to head back down the path towards the basement door.

"You should try it sometime," Zoe called after me.

I turned around. "Try what?"

"Facing what scares you. It's the only way you can truly be yourself."

"Thanks for the tip, Dr. Phil," I said sarcastically.

"I'm serious. Why'd you think I dared you to go to Sterling Creek Forest?"

"What? I don't know. You were trying to come up with the coolest dare ever?"

"No," she replied. "'Cause I think it'd be neat to be friends with someone who went in the forest and lived to tell what's there. Plus, you could show me your scratches and cuts too! Want to see mine? They're not from the forest but they're almost as good." Zoe gave one of her crazy giggles which sounded like chuckling and blowing her nose at the same time.

"No thanks," I said. I hope she doesn't think of me as a friend because I don't ever see that happening.

When I got back inside, I knelt down and opened my backpack. I took out a t-shirt and managed to dry most of my arms, legs and feet. I climbed on to the air mattress and settled in. In my mind, I kept replaying what had happened earlier in the night with Zoe's dare and her sitting outside as if waiting for some sign or spirit or something. *Why do people do strange things?* I wondered. *Are they tired of the way so-called 'normal' people behave and try to do things just to be different? Or maybe I'm the weird one and Zoe's normal?* I couldn't figure it out.

I used my left hand to make sure my pendant and chain were connected properly and then touched the back of my neck to make sure it wasn't loose. I buried my head deep into my pillow and slowly drifted off to sleep. Aside from the pendant scare and Zoe's weird behaviour, the sleepover at Linh's was fun. I decided to hold off on telling her about how Zoe wandered outside in the middle of the night. Maybe I will tell her some other time.

I got home at around twelve the next afternoon and worked on some Language Arts questions that were due on Monday. I then turned on the TV and caught the end of Ranger Rick. It's my favourite show about this guy dressed up as a park ranger who teaches you about animals and habitats. This episode was a re-run but I watched it anyway. Sometimes you miss stuff on a show or in a song or book the first time you go through it but then you notice things the second or third time. I didn't notice anything new this time because I dozed off during the final scenes.

Dad came from upstairs and I sat up trying to shake off the sleepiness. I rubbed my eyes and headed over to the kitchen. As promised, he started preparing the chicken wings. I helped him brush and season them and before I knew it, we were taking them out of the oven and waiting for them to cool down. Dad made some pasta salad to go with the wings while I cut up some cucumbers and put them on a plate. He looked over my shoulder as I finished the last few.

"Looking good!" he said.

"Thanks."

As I watched him mix, taste and turn the heat down, I couldn't help but think about how much I loved him. I think I only use that word when I think about animals or my dad. Not only did he make sure I was taken care of but he always kept his promises. I can't remember a time when he said he'd do something and never followed through. I wouldn't have cared if we weren't able to try out his wing recipe today because I know he'd make it up to me another way. I wish my mom felt this way too. Maybe she did. I decided to try and find out after some mouthfuls of pasta had been swallowed and small chicken bones piled up in a corner of my plate.

"Do you ever think about mom?" I asked him.

"Sure. Quite often, actually," he replied, wiping his mouth with a sheet of paper towel.

"Do you think she'll ever come back and live with us?"

Dad paused and slowly moved his lips around. Either something was caught in his teeth or he was acting like a cartoon character trying to come up with a plan.

"I don't know. Why?"

"I'm just wondering why we never hear from her. I know the two of you didn't get along but she's still my mom. I miss her." My throat felt dry. I took a sip of juice and that helped a little.

He dragged his chair close to me and touched my forearm. "I know it's hard. Believe me, I've tried calling her. I kept thinking, 'You don't have to say anything to me but please pick up for Dhanika. Talk to her, even if it's just for a minute.' Nothing. No answer." He closed his eyes for a moment.

I felt tears taking over my eyes but wanted to look strong in front of dad. I wiped them away with the back of my hand. "So, she doesn't like me anymore?"

"No, she still loves you, like I do."

"She doesn't!" I snapped, raising my voice. "If she cared, she should show it! Look how nice you are to me. You care, you're fun and you never break a promise. Why can't she see that?"

"She did see that. It was just a whole set of other things we couldn't agree on," he told me.

I looked down and rested my chin on my hand. I didn't know what else to say.

"It's not fair. I see Linh and her mom and all these other moms with their kids and want mine to be around so I can be just like them!"

Dad pulled me close to him and I pressed my head on his shoulder. He didn't say anything but I knew he wanted to pull out my sadness and pain and toss them away as far as he could.

"You're the best dad in the world," I quietly told him. "It's just sometimes, I wish I had a mom."

"I know." He gently pulled me up and gave me a hug. Then he kissed me on the forehead. "You want to go out and do something?"

"No, that's okay, dad, thanks," I said. "I'm meeting Linh

later on. We're going for a bike ride." I helped tidy up before I left the house.

I guarded the bikes outside the convenience store at Ridgemount Plaza. Linh and I have bike locks, but we don't really trust them. We worry that some thief is going to come along with giant cutters and snap the locks in two. I couldn't put up much of a fight against someone bigger and stronger than I but vowed to go down swinging trying to protect my bike. I look at it thinking, 'Who wouldn't want this bike?' It's a shiny blue, Hatchford 250 with beautiful handlebars and spokes. Sometimes I pretend I am pedalling a fancy car when I ride it through the neighbourhood.

Linh and I rode over to the community centre balancing our freezies in our left hands. Mine was blue and Linh's was orange. We wobbled down the path and then on to some grass where we got off and stood our bikes on their kickstands. We sat on the grass and began to attack our frozen treats.

"Ah. So nice!" Linh said.

"Yeah," I agreed. "Perfect day for this."

It was true. This Saturday afternoon was a hot one for late May. It felt more like July or August. I squeezed the plastic and some frozen blue goodness inched up towards the opening at the top.

"Good idea getting the freezies cut at the store," I told her.

"Yeah," she replied. "I hate biting off the top with my teeth!"

I looked around at the community centre building and the nearby park and tennis courts. They were all being used and the people who were in or near them seemed happy and full of life. I felt the same way.

Linh continued. "You have to cut freezies the right way. You can't just snip off the tops. Cutting them in a 'u' shape is the best. That way you don't slice the inside of your mouth when you eat it."

"Some people need the inside of their mouth to get jabbed a little," I said, immediately thinking of Zoe. "That might shut them up." We both laughed.

"Hey, look at that over there," I said pointing to some taller grass.

"What?" asked Linh.

"Something's moving."

"Really? I don't see it."

"Here, hold this for a sec," I told her, handing over my melting blue freezie. "I'm going to check it out."

I walked over and discovered a small brown and white rabbit that was twitching. Every time it tried to run, it would wince and move around in circles. Linh joined me about a minute later.

"What's going on?" she asked.

"This rabbit's hurt. Where's Ranger Rick when you need him?"

"You want me to get help while you wait here with it?"

"No, that's okay. I think I see the problem. It's his back leg." I stroked the rabbit and petted it to try and make it less afraid. He seemed to calm down a bit.

"There's something stuck in it," I explained. "I'm going to try and get it out."

"Okay. Be careful," warned Linh.

Through its damp fur, I felt something rough and prickly. I pulled and out came a clump of thorns and leaves. I threw it away into the grass along with some flecks of blood. I looked down at my thumb and index finger and noticed some small cuts. I found an old, linty tissue in my pocket and held it tightly.

"The rabbit's leaving!" Linh told me.

"What? He can't! There's something else that's not right. We have to get him to a vet," I said.

We rushed back to our bikes and pedalled after the rabbit.

He had a big lead on us but we were gaining on him. Then he paused, looked around and twitched his nose, just before running under the opening of a large fence.

Linh and I came to a skidding stop. The tall fence stood before us folding its imaginary, iron arms as if daring us to go past. The sign with capital letters was almost shouting its warning:

'NO TRESPASSING BY ORDER OF THE CITY OF STERLING CREEK AND THE POLICE DEPARTMENT.'

"We have to find that rabbit," I told her.

"What? Are you crazy? I'm too young to have a funeral!"

"But think about what'll happen to him if he's not healed properly. Some bigger animals will get him," I said.

"And if we go in there, some big, scary thing's going to get us!"

"It's still light out," I reminded her. "We'll go in and look around. If we don't find him after a while, we'll just leave."

"The cops are always checking..."

"No one's around now. If we go in quickly and come out, nobody will even notice!" I said.

"I don't know..." Linh said, shuddering. "What if we went back to the community centre and asked..."

But it was too late. I had already pushed my bike under the opening in the fence and squeezed my way through. I pedalled towards some bushes, brushed them aside and entered the thick forest.

Chapter 6
Forbidden Territory

The forest was cool and mostly shady and damp. Tall trees with their bent, leafy branches seemed to hug everything around them. The stories about this place, so far, seemed untrue. This so-called haunted, evil forest was quite the opposite. The pleasant odour of rich garden soil and warm greenhouse-like air seemed to be filling my nostrils. To tell you the truth, I felt more relaxed and at ease than I thought I would.

My eyes shifted around in search of the injured rabbit. *Where could he have gone?* I wondered. Everything was so dense and the forest floor was rough and bumpy, which made it tricky and difficult to bike. Eventually I dismounted and steered my bike using the handgrips.

"Dhanika!" a voice called from the distance.

Must be Linh, I thought. "Over here!" I replied. "Follow my voice!"

Linh found me a few minutes later. I noticed that she was able to bike on the uneven ground though she twisted and turned. Maybe it was on the lowest gear or something. Linh came to a wobbling stop beside me.

"Are you nuts? This place is so scary! Let's get out of here!" she said.

"Just a minute," I told her. "I need to find that rabbit!"

"How? Do you see the size of this place?"

"Yeah, I know." I paused and looked up. The sun's rays were shining through the trees like a bright summer morning. Was something magical about to happen?

Linh continued. "You saw how fast he is. And even if we do find him, what are we going to do then?"

"I'll take him to a vet," I said. "How else is he going to get there? The bunny ambulance doesn't come to these parts! Now help me look."

Linh took a deep breath of frustration and exhaled. "How do we even get him over to us? Say 'Here fluffy, here?'"

"Just make a whistling sound and keep your eyes open," I offered.

"Whistle? It's not a lost dog!"

"Well, think of something else then! I'm going that way. You look over there and we'll meet back here in ten minutes." We walked off in opposite directions.

My bike stood slanted on its kickstand as I walked towards some bushes. Before I entered, I spent a few minutes gathering some small stones. I made my way through the bushes and walked across the mounds of soil and weeds. Branches cracked and snapped under my feet and twigs lightly scratched my arms with their pointy ends. I pushed aside some branches remembering to drop a stone every minute or so. That way, I'd be able to find my way back to the clearing to meet Linh.

I used all of my senses trying to spot monsters or strange creatures before they got me. The daylight really helped. There were fewer shadows where they could hide. I began wondering what I would do if I came across some weird, angry monster the other kids swore they had seen in this forest. I wouldn't be able to run and if I hid, it would probably find me. Should I throw something at it? That might work. Maybe if I made an ugly face, the creature or whatever it was would get scared and run. Yes, that's it! It wouldn't know what to do when faced with the opposite of what was expected. That's what Mr. Stellick was calling 'irony,' in Language Arts class the other day. He said an easy way to remember irony was to think of it as "the old switcheroo."

As I walked through the trees and bushes, I practised making different scary faces. They must have worked on some squirrels because they made some clicking sounds and dashed off behind some logs. I wish I had a mirror to see what my scary faces looked like. The rest of the forest did not seem to be afraid. It continued its swaying and rustling and usual forest sounds.

At first, I thought the flowing water was rain. *Please don't be a thunderstorm*, I thought. Then it occurred to me that rain doesn't just start off with buckets of water being overturned on the ground or in the sky. It starts off slowly as drops then comes down light or hard. *Silly girl*, I thought to myself. *Keep going!* As I continued walking, the water sound grew louder. Must be some lake or river... Sterling Creek! That had to be it.

I walked towards the sound. The bushes and leaves thinned out and I found myself on the edge of a small clearing with a large creek before me. The water looked so clear and pure as it bubbled over the greyish-brown rocks and moss. Maybe Mr. Bunny came here to take a drink. I scanned the riverbanks and nearby bushes but saw no sign of any animal. Then my eyes travelled across the creek to the other side where the forest continued. What was that in the bushes over there? A little head jerked from side to side and its nose twitched. Definitely a rabbit but was it the one that I had helped earlier?

I decided to find out. I know rabbits are afraid of bodies of water so how did it get over on that side? I looked out on the river and discovered that there were several large rocks that were scattered across the width of the river. They looked slippery but big enough to cross. I would have to take my time. I hopped to the first one and then the next. I almost lost my balance on the last one and ended up flinging the remaining rocks I was carrying into the river. I watched as they danced and bobbed with the current. Now there would be no way to trace my route. Oh well. I would just have to remember to come back to these big rocks. If I made it back to the other side of the river from where I came at least there were small rocks that I had dropped to help me retrace my steps.

My wet feet and socks made a squelching sound as I hopped off the rocks and made my way into the forest on the other side of the river. The trees and shrubs were just as thick on this side but it was a bit easier to walk among the bushes and branches. I spotted squirrels, chipmunks and birds but there was no sign of rabbits. I felt a little silly moving around in a forest with my feet soaked chasing a silly rabbit but as I made my way deeper into it, the less afraid I became. I could understand how those who entered this forest at night were afraid but it seemed pretty nice during the day. And what were those grave markers the other kids and teenagers spoke about? I sure didn't see any. Maybe there were large rocks that looked like tombstones at night. But I had nothing to worry about, did I? The sun was still out and some clouds were moving in. I also noticed that the air had become cooler—a nice change to the heat that forced Linh and me to stop for freezies earlier in the afternoon.

I decided to walk up ahead to a mini ravine where there was a bit of a slope on the forest floor. That's when I felt a drop on my arm. At first, I was worried that it was bird poop but there were no white spots on my arm. Once when I was in Grade Three, I spilled some whiteout on my hand at school. A couple of boys and girls laughed thinking that a bird did its business on me. It was a tough stain to get out and I remember the whole incident bothered me for a while until my teacher told me not to worry. She explained that getting hit with bird droppings was supposed to be good luck.

Suddenly my arms were wet and I wished it had been bird droppings and not water. The clouds slowly became darker and the wind grew angrier. I felt more droplets on my arm and knew that it would pour any minute. *What should I do? I wondered. I'll get soaked before I make it through these bushes and stuff back to the river where I have to cross those big rocks and then follow my Hansel and Gretel trail back to my bike. My bike! It's going to get soaked!* I hoped the tall trees around it would absorb most of the rain in their branches and leaves.

A bright flash shot across the sky. My heart raced. I was in the second most dangerous place in the world for a thunderstorm. Being out in an open lake or river was definitely the worst. But sitting underneath big trees wasn't far behind. What if lightning hit those lanky things and they split and came crashing down on me? Talk about needing the bunny ambulance!

I had to find shelter that would not injure me if lightning struck. I rushed towards the edge of the ravine and slid down. It wasn't that steep. There were some thick bushes straight ahead which seemed good enough for protection. I ran towards them and crouched underneath as the thunder boomed overhead. I covered my ears but there was rain and heavy wind all around me. I inched farther into the bushes and suddenly my hand touched what felt like...

No. A sheet of glass? *It can't be,* I thought. *Out here in the middle of the forest?*

I felt around some more and discovered that there were thick, grimy logs on either side of the glass. *How big is this thing?* I wondered. *What could it be? A house?*

It was a small structure covered with thick bushes and branches which made it impossible to see from a distance. I didn't even notice it standing on the edge of the ravine. That's how well it was hidden.

I decided to remain crouched with my back against the

logs. I had enough sense not to even think about entering this strange cabin, house or whatever it was. I was pretty comfortable for the moment and would wait for the storm to pass before I made my way back. I hoped that Linh found her own shelter or managed to get away.

I waited for what seemed like an hour. The storm weakened and I was almost ready to leave when curiosity nudged me.

I pressed my face against the dirty, smudged window and looked inside. The place was cluttered with junk – books, a radio, an old TV, cans, jars and a couple of old chairs. There was also some...

A quick scream of terror escaped my lips as a hunched figure darted across the room.

Chapter 7

A Pinky Promise

I jumped back from the window with my hand to my mouth. I tried to control my breathing, refusing to believe what I just saw. What was someone or something doing in a tiny house in the middle of a forbidden forest? Does it live in this place? Would it chase me? And how did it even get here?

I was trapped. I couldn't run away and hide in the middle of a thunderstorm but what choice did I have? I wasn't going to stick around near a strange, old house with some crazy thing running around inside!

Think! What should I do? I brushed away a strand of wet hair from my eyes.

Skreeeee... Skreeeee...

What was that sound?

Skreeee...

There it was again!

Was it coming from that house? I shut my eyes tightly and plugged my ears, expecting an explosion.

When I did not hear a loud bang, I opened my eyes. The house was still there but the windows had some strange markings. When I moved a few steps closer, I saw that the marks were words written in the dust, probably with a finger.

They read:

SAVE YOURSELF. COME TO ME.

What did that even mean? Save who? Was the thing inside going to give me an umbrella because I sure could use one in this downpour! I wasn't even sure if the message was for me. Was it for someone else? No, it couldn't have been. I remember walking around the little house and never hearing that screeching sound through any of the walls or windows.

I had enough sense to know that I shouldn't go into any strange house, especially one in the middle of a dangerous forest no children were allowed to enter. Still, though, I was curious about what or who was inside. Maybe the inside of the house would explain the message on the window. Excitement and fear were building up inside making my stomach feel funny.

I thought back to two times I had this exact feeling. Once when I first heard about scary things inside Sterling Creek Forest and the other time when dad and I baked a chocolate cake and I ended up licking more of the leftover batter from the bowl than I should have. I had to sip some ginger ale and lie down until my stomach settled.

The chipped, wooden front door slowly opened. My breathing quickened again and I stood where I was, unsure whether to run or watch. A thin hand emerged with an index finger that curled and uncurled inviting me in. My mouth dropped and my eyes and ears quivered. It was as though I was out in the middle of a winter blizzard. Other parts of me twitched and at times I couldn't feel the ground beneath me.

Suddenly I returned to my senses and decided what to do. I didn't want to do anything in or near a strange house by myself so I found enough courage to cup my hand to my mouth and shout, "Not today! Maybe later!" Then I turned and ran through the bushes from where I came, heading towards the river back to Linh.

The rain became lighter as I crossed the large rocks and

found my trail of rock 'breadcrumbs' that led me back to my bike. It was soaked but still standing by the time I got to the clearing. I found a couple of leaves nearby and wiped the seat which got rid of most of the water.

After some wandering and calling out, I came across Linh near some rocks by the edge of the forest. She too was soaked but glad to see me.

"Dhanika! What happened to you? I was so worried!" she said.

"I saw the rabbit across the river on the other side of the forest," I explained. "But by the time I crossed, he was gone! Then the rain started."

"You're nuts!" Linh exclaimed. "You put us through all this trouble just for some rabbit?"

"You could've left," I reminded her.

"But I didn't want to leave you alone out here. We could've gotten killed! Let's just go!"

We walked our bikes out of the forest and down the muddy trail. Thankfully there was no one brave enough standing guard by the fence that separated the community from Sterling Creek forest so we wiggled our way under and were soon riding home.

We pedalled on the rain-darkened sidewalks going through puddles. As we went along, I vowed not to say anything about the little house and the finger thing. I lasted about eight minutes and couldn't take it anymore. Linh was riding in front of me when I called out to her.

"I saw something in the forest."

"Oh yeah? Another rabbit?"

"No, something else. A weird, little house."

"You're joking, right?" Linh asked. She slowed down and we both stopped by a curb.

"No, I'm serious."

"How serious?"

I looked right at her brown eyes as I pulled the chain up from under my shirt to my chin. "I swear on this pendant," I told her with a straight face. Her eyes widened. She knew I meant business.

"So what did you see?" asked Linh.

"When I was looking to get out of the rain, I found this house. Kind of a like a mini cabin that was hidden by bushes and trees and stuff. Very easy to miss."

"Wow! Was anyone in there?"

"Yeah. Some weird, little thing ran across the room. Then there was a message written on the window inviting me in to save myself, whatever that means," I told her.

"Save yourself?" repeated Linh. "Sounds like a life jacket store!"

I laughed and continued. "I didn't go in to find out, even after this skinny little hand curled its finger beckoning me to go in."

Linh shuddered. "Ugh. So creepy!"

I was silent for a moment. "Do you think that little house is the reason the kids are told to stay away from the forest?" I asked her.

"I don't know," Linh replied. "That's so weird. Kind of like something out of a fairy tale."

"Yeah," I agreed. "I should take a look at some of those old fairy tales. I think I still have a book of them on my shelf!"

"Okay," Linh said. "And then after we tell the police about..."

"Wait, wait. Hold on," I interrupted. "Tell the police?"

"Yeah. We can't have some strange, little house in the forest near where we live with who-knows-what in it!"

"No, no," I objected. "We aren't telling anyone anything!"

"What?" cried Linh. "We have to! What if there's some zombie up in that house that comes out at night and wipes out the neighbourhood?"

"Don't be silly," I told her. "I don't think there's any zombie in there!"

"But you don't know there isn't!" argued Linh.

"Look, I chose to tell you about that house," I reminded her. "I didn't have to tell you anything but I did because you're my friend and I trust you. So now you have to promise to keep what I told you a secret until we can figure out what it is."

"We?" asked Linh. "You and me?"

"Yeah. Promise?"

Linh looked down for a moment. I moved closer to her.

"Come on," I encouraged.

She and I slowly interlocked two small fingers.

"Pinky promise," we both said. We continued biking down the wet sidewalk.

Chapter 8

A Meeting in May

The newspaper club meets every Tuesday and Thursday after school. The meetings take place in the art room at the back, close to the storage room where all of the brushes, paint and art supplies are kept. The room is clean and bright and has a unique smell of ink and paint but not the kind that makes you cough. The large tables are perfect for scattering drawings of ideas and laying out papers as we write and design. Sometimes we open one of the four metallic-framed windows if it's not too cold outside but they are usually closed when we work.

The newspaper is called The Meadow Monthly because it's finished near the end of the month. It is sold outside the lunchroom on the second last or last day of the month for two dollars. If you ask me, that's a pretty good deal. The Meadow Monthly is about five to six pages long and is actually quite interesting. It has puzzles, quizzes, a joke page and those silly spot-the-difference pictures where you have to look at what is different about two pictures that look almost the same. Along with the fun stuff, there are articles about events at the school, interviews with teachers and students and photographs of trips, trophies and medals won at tournaments and competitions.

One of my favourite sections in the magazine is called

'What If?' Students submit opinions that imagine what the school would be like if certain changes were made. They are also allowed to send in drawings or photos to go with their articles. We remind them that we usually shrink the pictures in order to put everything together properly. Here are some examples of stuff students actually handed in. Some were printed but most weren't:

What if we asked the school board to have classes on Saturday and Sunday in order to make summer vacation longer?

What if two of the hallway water fountains were turned into orange pop machines?

What if we had a 'Build Your Own Burger Day,' rather than boring pizza days?

What if we could get The Eight By Tens (a popular boy band) to perform at our next school dance?

Of course none of these ideas was ever put into place, but it was still funny to read people's arguments for or against a particular idea. A boy in Grade 7 wrote that candy should be sold after lunch to fight bad breath. I remember thinking, *What a terrible idea. The last thing some of these spazzes need is more sugar. They're crazy enough without the candy!*

Derek Thompson, a tall, lanky boy in Grade 8, is the student editor and our staff supervisor is Derek's social studies teacher Mrs. Francine. One thing I like about her is that she rarely interrupts or forces her ideas on us. She lets the group debate and argue and reminds us to "challenge and attack ideas, not people."

We do a good job being nice to each other most of the time but disagree every now and then on different suggestions and topics. There are a little over a dozen students who help put together The Monthly Meadow. Each grade level has about five students who come up with ideas for articles, take pictures and review things that other students would like to see printed. Sometimes the Grade 8 students try to take over with their opinions about what's good and what isn't, but Mrs. Francine tells them that "all contributions and voices need to be considered, no matter what grade or age."

One Thursday afternoon in May, the newspaper club was discussing some last-minute jokes that needed to be added to the puzzles and jokes page. I sorted through a few creased sheets of jokes that I shared with the group but they weren't impressed.

"Is that supposed to be funny?" a Grade 8 girl asked.

"Yeah," I said. "I like it."

"Maybe like Grade 6 kids find it funny, but that's kinda lame," added a boy, also in Grade 8. "Got anything else?"

There were no other jokes submitted so I thought back for a moment to some of the silly stuff Linh and I say to each other. I picked up a pen, turned one of the sheets over and wrote. I looked up. "How about this?" I asked the group:

"Q – What did Cinderella say after her picture was taken?

A – Some day my prints will come."

The students groaned and rolled their eyes.

"Cinderella? Really? What are we, like in Kindergarten?"

"Yeah, I don't think so!"

"We're trying to get people to read the paper not burn it!"

"I thought it was good," I told them, suddenly feeling like I had shrunk. *What does it take to impress people around here? I thought. The way things were going, I'll have to start paying people to be my friend!* I was happy that I had made friends with Linh and Sarah but man, why was everyone too cool to laugh and call stuff babyish? It was a strange feeling. On one hand, I wanted to be accepted and often wondered what it would be like to be friends with some of the older girls but at the same time I was, for the most part, happy with who I was.

I turned to Mrs. Francine for support. She looked up, but stayed put at her desk. Her smile quickly disappeared.

"Don't be mean," she warned the students. "Put Dhanika's idea aside for now. Go back to it later if you need to," she advised.

Derek placed it on top of a folder in front of him. "This is the second last Monthly of the year," he reminded us. "We want to end on a high note. I don't want any more problems creeping up on us."

I thought things were fine with the newspaper. I was curious so I spoke up.

"What kinds of problems?"

Using his thumbnail, he scratched below his nose. "The Monthly doesn't sell as well as it used to," he told us. "Students don't seem to care about what's going on around here. They want to see and read stuff that's new and interesting not just articles and stories about things they already know."

Derek opened his folder and pulled out a newspaper from March. "Look at this," he instructed, holding up the front page. "'Grade 8 Boys' Volleyball Team Serves Up Second Championship,'" he read. "By the time The Monthly got out, everyone knew about this for two weeks. It was old news!"

We were silent.

Nathan, a Grade 7 student, offered a suggestion. "Let's take a look at what our best issues of The Monthly were and then we can use what worked when we..."

"We don't have time for that," Derek interrupted. "The school year's almost over. There are tests, report cards and grad all coming up. June's a busy month. We know what's good and what isn't. The puzzles, jokes and stuff can stay. He shot me a quick glance. "Dhanika, even that silly one you dropped on us a minute ago might get printed."

I folded my arms and sat back satisfied.

He went on. "But the writing and articles have to be better. No more old news!" He slapped his hand on the table to add to his point. "We need to work together to make

The Monthly the best paper. Something that has news and information students can't get anywhere else!"

Derek closed the folder in front of him. "We're meeting again next Tuesday. Between now and then, come up with something to present at the next meeting that we can put in the paper. We can do this, guys!"

He reminded me of a sports coach trying to inspire his players to step up and win the game. I left the meeting wondering if I would be able to come up with an article and maybe even a cool picture by next Tuesday. At least my Cinderella riddle had a chance of making the jokes page.

But it wasn't the same as getting invited to the ball.

Joss left shortly after I ate dinner. It was around 6:30 and dad would be home by 8:30. The house was quiet and I used that time to finish a science project. I had to design three structures with good, average and poor stability. I only needed to make a sturdy bridge because I already finished a house built on posts and a wobbly lookout tower. Everything was held down by a combination of clear and masking tape on bristol board. I balanced it carefully down the stairs and eased it on to the table in our living room.

I looked at how cluttered the room seemed even though I only added my project. And it wasn't even taking up too much space. My thoughts immediately jumped to the last time I saw a cluttered room. I was on the outside looking in a cabin that I definitely didn't want to enter. But the message on that window about saving me still had me wondering. What did it mean? And why did I have to go to her to get saved? Why couldn't she just shout out the instructions or e-mail them to me?

I went up to my room and took out a pen and my green mini notebook. I sat with my back against the bed head and pulled my knees up forming a mountain shape. I began writing as much as I could about what I saw in the forest the day Linh and I got soaked. I came up with four important notes:

1. I have to go back to Sterling Creek Forest with or without Linh. There's some mystery in there that needs to be solved.
2. The fences around Sterling Creek Forest aren't always guarded. But when exactly is there no one standing guard?
3. That little cabin might be part of the reason children are told to stay out of Sterling Creek Forest.
4. The woman or thing inside the cabin is not out to hurt me. If she wanted to, she would have attacked me when I was there. What does she want with me?

It was almost as if whatever was in the cabin had chosen me to do or say something. I needed to know what it was.

The clock radio near my bed showed 7:12. There was more than enough time to head over to the forest and get back in time before it became dark and dad got home. I quickly looked out my window. It was still pretty bright outside. There were even people on the sidewalk playing, talking or walking their dogs.

I leaped out of bed, rushed downstairs and quickly stuffed my feet in my shoes. I double knotted the laces and charged out the door, locking it behind me. A moment later the automatic door opener was churning and whirring behind me as the garage door curved over and fell like a waterfall as it closed. I pedalled furiously down the street. If I had not been wearing shorts, my pants would have gotten tangled in the chain and I would have been sent tumbling to the road.

The early evening air was cool as I made my way to the forest. I was glad I was on my way to find out more about the cabin. I was excited that Linh and I were the only ones who knew about this place. We were also among a handful of young people who had entered and crossed Sterling Creek. I wished she were with me now but didn't have the time to stop by her house and wait until she got ready.

As the forest grew nearer, I became nervous. I looked around for any adult patrols or police officers behind the community centre or near the opening in the fence Linh and I had used the last time. There didn't seem to be anyone nearby. Entering the forbidden forest was not the only reason I was afraid. I kept thinking, *what if the thing inside the cabin doesn't have long to live and needs to tell me some secrets?*

I pushed my bike up to the fence and slid under the opening. I reached back and was about to pull my bike in with me when a big voice bellowed:

"Stop! Right there!"

Another voice called out, "Keep going and you'll lose the bike and your life!"

I looked through the chain link fence. Rats! Actually, this was worse than that.

It was the police.

Chapter 9

Train with Weirs

I froze. Should I put my hands up like the bad guys on TV? No, that's silly. But I broke a rule, didn't I? Would they tell dad what happened? Worse, would I go to jail for the rest of my life? I found it hard to breathe and was beginning to sweat. I didn't even bother trying to wipe my forehead.

Maybe I'll put one hand up and that'll make the cops less angry with me.

Wait, raise my hand? What is this, Period 6 Math? No, you fool, think!

I had never been in trouble like this in my life. Sometimes at school, teachers would warn me with a sharp voice to stop talking during group work. And at home, when I was little, mom and dad would get angry when I would do the opposite of what they asked but this was different. Teachers and parents don't have guns and handcuffs. And running away or crying was not going to work with these officers.

I felt my body quivering. Instead of above my head, I raised both hands near my shoulders, trying to be the nicest bad girl they had ever seen. The two police officers moved closer and stood right beside me. I looked up and turned my head to the left.

"What's your name?" the female officer asked.

Just give them what always works—the truth.

"D...Dhanika," I quietly answered.

"Dhanika, what does that big white sign on that big fence say in big black letters?" she asked sarcastically.

"No... No trespassing."

"Speak up! Can't hear you."

"No trespassing," I said a bit louder.

"What do you think that means?" asked the male officer.

Sweat tickled my forehead. "Don't go past something," I told him.

"So, what were you doing past the fence?"

"Getting my rabbit. He got hurt and ran that way and I went after him." That was sort of the truth, right?

The officers stepped away from me and began whispering. I barely made out the words "troublemaker" and "first time." They returned sooner than I thought. I tightened up nervously wondering what would happen next. Beads of sweat formed on my back and forehead. Wasn't perspiration supposed to cool people down? It didn't seem to be working because waves of heat surged through my entire body. I was sure I was on fire.

"Pick up your bike, get back on that path and go home," the female officer instructed. "If you ever come around here again, there'll be consequences. We know your name and what you look like."

"And wear a helmet when you're riding," the other officer said. "Now you have two warnings against you. We won't tell your parents this time but if you decide to break any more rules or laws, you'll be getting a lift home in our cruiser. Got it?"

"Yes."

I decided that this wouldn't be the best time to tell them that I lived only with dad. The officers stood with folded arms as I picked up my bike and pedalled towards the path and community centre. They watched until I was out of sight.

My breathing returned to normal and I stopped sweating but could not push the officers' anger out of my mind. The police seemed so much friendlier when they visited schools and classrooms and made presentations about stranger awareness and bicycle safety. They would smile, answer questions and hand out Calvin the Crime Dog stickers and activity booklets. Police officers look and sound differently when you break a rule and make them angry. Was I a bad person for getting in trouble? And would dad ever find out? I decided there was no way I could ever tell him what just happened. The last thing I wanted was to make dad upset or disappointed in me.

There were still bits of sun out as it began to duck behind the distant trees and buildings. Thank goodness I made it back home just before 8:30. Dad still was not home which made me feel relieved since I wasn't in the mood to answer more grown-up questions. I left the fridge door open as I drank some orange juice but that didn't take away the officers' angry voices that swirled around in my head. The quivering returned and inched its way up to my face. Leaning against the sink, I tried to stop the tears but it was too late. Sometimes words hit harder than fists. They stay with you for a long time and just when you think you've gotten over something they punch and twist their way inside and not even the world's best chocolate cake or most awesome song can stop the pain.

The tears kept coming. I cried because I got in trouble with scary police officers who had a secret on me that they could tell the world whenever they felt like it. I cried because I had no warm shoulder near me on which I could rest my head and dry my wet face. No hugs or pats on the shoulder came when I needed them most. Maybe I didn't deserve them.

I washed my face in the bathroom, brushed my teeth and got into bed. Normally, I'm up when dad gets home but I couldn't face him tonight. I turned off my light and lay in the darkness on my bed. I heard him moving around downstairs a few minutes later. He called my name but I didn't answer. Later, when he opened my door, I pretended to be asleep.

That night was difficult and restless. I tried moving my eyes around quickly, hoping it would make me sleepy. When that didn't work, I read using a flashlight just in case dad got up and looked for any light at the bottom of my door. I barely remembered anything from the three and a half chapters I read.

I closed my book and quietly walked over to the closet. I pulled out Thomas, my stuffed bear and got back into bed. I hugged him tightly and began to feel tired. That is the nice thing about stuffed animals. They don't say mean things or get angry. They just let you feel their softness as you hug or rub your face against them. On that sad night, I hugged Thomas harder than I ever did in my life and then turned towards my window. Through an opening in the curtains, I looked out at the tiny stars sprinkled on the dark night sky and wondered if anyone else at this very moment was feeling the same way. I reached under my shirt and touched the corners of each letter on my pendant.

Where are you, mom?

***

It is amazing what sleep can do. I felt better when I woke up the next morning. The police officers' words felt lighter and hurt less. It was Friday too, so that helped. I even had a pretty good day at school. Things are more easygoing in the hallways and classrooms by the end of the week. Teachers wear jeans and t-shirts and seem friendlier. They joke around more than usual and I think I know why. One Friday, I caught a glimpse of the counter in the staff room. It was full of snacks and treats and I was sure they had a lot to do with the teachers' good moods. Full stomachs make everyone happy.

The weekend everyone seemed to look forward to so

much, erased any cheer. Saturday greeted Sterling Creek with thundering, smoky grey skies. Heavy rain flooded gutters which overflowed, spewing water, tiny stones and dirt down the sides of houses. The streets and sidewalks reflected the rainwater as it hit the ground.

Joss was off for the weekend and dad got called to an emergency meeting at work. I kept busy by playing a computer game called Grocery Grab. You have to steer your cart through different sections of a grocery store and pick up healthy foods and throw out the junk food. You have to avoid crashing into other shopping carts or store workers stocking the shelves. I can never beat the enemy at the final stage which is confronting the angry store manager. The game is okay. I wasn't really concentrating on it.

A pop-up ad appeared in the right corner. It was advertising Weir's self-defence classes. Their slogan was, "Train with Weirs and face your fears."

Face your fears...

Something happened at that moment. I looked out the window. It was still raining but I felt a longing and excitement. I had left something unfinished a couple of days ago and no longer wanted to be held back by thunder and lightning or tough police officers. Was it something from the computer that gave me these feelings? Could it have been a jolt of bravery like a lightning bolt? Or maybe Zoe was somewhere sticking pins in her Dhanika doll. I put the computer on sleep mode and quickly slipped on my boots and rain jacket. Making sure all the doors were locked, I went into the garage and pulled out an old green crate. Underneath an air pump and gloves, I found a bike helmet I used to wear. I snapped the chin strap button in place and discovered it was a bit tight but at least I was protected. I pulled my hood over the helmet, got on my bike and headed towards the community centre.

I avoided getting too close to the fence this time. I rode

around the path, probably longer than I should have, looking for any patrols. There was no one, just like the first time Linh and I visited the forest and the weather was bad. Lucky me. I was counting on the thunderstorm to keep any grownups away from the fence.

I slid under the fence, pulled my bike with me and headed up the muddy trail. Inside the forest, I came across the clearing where I had left my bike the last time. I activated the kickstand and left it under a shelter of thick branches.

A few minutes later, I jumped from one large rock to the other and made it across the river and soon found myself sliding down the small ravine on the other side of the forest. When I hit the bottom with a soft thud, I realized that coming here might have been a mistake. The rain didn't seem to have lessened. In fact, it had become windier and colder and thunder rumbled above. I was nervous. What if the cabin wasn't even here?

I walked over to the thick undergrowth and began pushing through to the other side. I felt the dusty glass and bent down a little. The faded message was still there:

SAV YO RSELF. COM TO ME.

Suddenly the hidden front door swung open and I heard a voice inside:

"Come in, Dhanika. I knew you'd return."

Chapter 10

The Woods are Watching

Children have people in their lives with whom they know what to do and say. Parents, babysitters and teachers respond to and even expect certain questions or comments from them. We spend most of our time learning which words work and which ones don't. You definitely should not speak to grownups the way you would when you are with your friends. For example, it would be strange to talk to dad the way Linh and I speak. I also found out the hard way that most of the time, what you say is as important as how you say it.

As I stood before this stranger standing in front of the cabin, it was difficult to figure out how to address her.

With the rain making rapid tapping sounds against my jacket, I slowly walked towards the open door from where I had heard the woman's voice. What was I going to say to her? And what did she mean by "expecting me?" That's something I'd heard on old black-and-white TV shows from people in suits and ties greeting their dinner guests. "Ah, my good chap. Do come in. I've been expecting you."

I stood in front of the doorway studying the woman. She was dressed in a grey hoodie, a bit taller than I but nothing like what I had imagined. I expected a thin, pale grandmother but she was younger than I thought. Her dark, stringy hair was tied neatly at the back with a strand that swung near one of her brown eyes. Her high cheekbones and a slightly smudged nose made it a little embarrassing for me to admit that I actually thought she was pretty. She just needed to wash her face a little.

I had that feeling someone gets when he or she is next in line to board a rollercoaster. Sure, it's frightening, maybe even to a point where you feel sick. But there is excitement too, knowing that you are about to go through something new or discover bravery you didn't realize you have. It wasn't easy being calm and I tried not to tremble or show any fear but still could not smile. Finally, I managed to speak:

"Hello."

"Hi Dhanika." Her voice was soft and soothing but I remained cautious.

"When... How? How do you know my name?"

"A girl called out to you the other day."

"You know Linh?"

"No. But words travel freely through the trees."

"So, you were spying on us?"

She gave a gentle laugh. "No, no. I heard her and then you found me. I saw you were looking around my home and didn't want to frighten you. So I wrote a message and had a feeling you'd come back."

This was too weird. The rainy Saturday, this forest and this woman who had been waiting for me to come back. Part of me wanted to turn and run back to my bike but another part of me wanted to find out more. I pointed to the doorway.

"Is this where you live?"

"Yes, that's it."

"Really? Out here in the forest by yourself?"

She nodded. "Would you like to see inside?"

I didn't answer. She moved closer to me and put her scratched, slightly darkened hand on mine. It was as soft as her voice.

"It's okay. I'm not going to hurt you, Dhanika. I actually need your help. We all need your help."

"What do you mean?"

She gave me a warm smile and headed to the cabin entrance. "Come and I'll show you."

Once you're in there, you may not come out, I thought to myself. *Be smart about this.* Out in the open, you can run away from traps but inside this gingerbread house is another...

As if she had read my mind, she said, with a hint of sadness, "Please. I don't mean to scare you but there isn't a lot of time. Just stand near the door if you're more comfortable with that."

That voice. There was something so kind about it, that you almost couldn't say no. "Okay," I told her. "But only for a minute."

I stepped in and looked around, taking in the earthy and pine scents that filled the cabin. There was only one level I could see and it was bigger and brighter than it looked from the outside. The dusty windows could have used a few squirts of window cleaner and a good wiping but other than that, the room was pretty nice. There were some old, wooden shelves that had jars and small boxes. A small table with a chair tucked in and a radio on top completed one corner and a bed and a small TV took up the other corner on the right. The wooden walls and floors were clean and almost shining. There was also a plastic basket with neatly folded clothes. As worn out as these things were, the place was surprisingly neat and tidy.

"Did you build this house?"

"No," she replied, moving aside a couple of boxes. "It's been standing here abandoned for decades. I just fixed it up a little."

"Wow," I said. "Is this all your stuff?"

"Most of it," she replied. "Some of it was being thrown out, like that TV I don't know why. It still works."

I looked at the shelves again. "What do you eat?"

"Spiders and worms mostly," she answered, with a straight face. "Mice and grasshoppers if it's a good week." She began to smile.

"Eww. Gross."

"I'm joking, Dhanika! Some things I eat come from the picnic sites around the community centre or the centre itself. It's amazing and sad what people throw out. I catch fish and get eggs from Willow Farm which only takes about fifteen..."

"What do you mean 'get eggs'?" I asked. "You steal them?"

She nodded. "But I only take what I need. And if I ever catch extra fish or pick fresh berries, I always go back and leave some at the farm house or for their cat."

I understood what she meant but it still seemed wrong to take something that did not belong to you. I looked around again and had to ask what I'm sure everyone was wondering.

"Where do you go to the bathroom?"

"If I'm out of the forest getting supplies, I sometimes use the one in the community centre. Other times, I go near the river. There's a part that has rocks that's behind a couple of maple trees. I set up a big bag under an opening on the rocks and all the waste goes in there. I either burn the waste or throw it out in garbage bins or in those big, steel disposal containers."

"Yuck!" I looked around and then behind me up towards the sky. It had stopped raining. I needed to go home but was still curious. "Is this your summer place? Do you have another house?"

"No, this is it. I got tired of the way I and other people lived—the pollution, the noise and always having to buy the next bit of technology. Humans are so wasteful. They love getting the newest toys and throwing things out. I wanted to leave all of that behind and just be alone with nature and not have anyone bother me. Everything I need is here. I have to borrow or get certain things but it's not a problem. The community centre has healthy living meetings twice a month. Anyone can attend and they give out free supplies like toothpaste, soap, bandages and other first aid things. I don't really need to buy anything."

"But it must be so lonely."

"Not really. I know people are around. I see and hear them in and around the community centre. And you'd be amazed how friendly animals can be."

"I know! I love all kinds of animals. I was trying to help a rabbit that got hurt. That's what led me into the forest." And just like that, I felt the distance between us shrink. It was as though a magical bridge popped up, sturdy and short enough to bring us together in the dense forest that afternoon. I could tell by the look on her face that she felt the same way.

"I'm so happy to hear you love animals!" she said, her voice rising a bit with excitement. "And you seem to like the outdoors as much as I do. I knew you were the right person to help us."

"Help who?"

"Everyone. You, the forest, the animals and the people of Sterling Creek, especially the young ones."

"Help them do what?"

She leaned towards me. Her scent was as attractive as she was. There was something magical and mysterious about this woman, yet I still did not trust her. But at least she was honest and answered every one of my questions. She spoke quietly, almost as if she were trying to keep the surrounding trees from listening.

"This forest has secrets, Dhanika. They're out there and most people don't know about them. I want to share them with you and hope that you'll do the right thing."

"What kind of secrets?"

"Words won't do it. I need to show them to you and it

looks like you want to get going."

"How'd you know?"

"Well, you're fidgeting and looking up at the sky. And I don't want to show and explain too much today. It's the first time we've actually spoken and I wanted you to find out a bit about me first. Come back in another day or two."

"I can't," I told her, remembering how scary it was with the police officers. "Kids aren't allowed in the forest. The fence on the outside is always guarded. I got in big trouble one time when I tried to get in."

She smiled. "It's okay. Don't worry about them. They might get angry and tell you to stay out but the truth is, those who try to keep children out are more afraid than you are. Sure, they might tell you it's dangerous in here and that you could die but they won't do anything bad to you."

I never thought of it that way and was happy to hear that. I felt relaxed. In fact, everything she told me today, except the forest secrets and bathroom part, put me at ease.

She gently took me by the arm. "I'll show you a place where you can get in and out of the forest without those bully patrols noticing."

"Thanks," I said. "But I have to get my bike first."

We walked away from the hidden cabin with her leading the way.

Biking home that afternoon gave me time to put together everything that had taken place in the forest. The woman in the cabin wasn't out to hurt me, just as I thought before I set out to meet her. I still had a bunch of questions. What was her life like before she moved into the forest? Did anyone else know she was there? And why did she choose me to keep the secrets of the forest? What was it about me that gave this woman the idea that I could be trusted? Other children and teenagers tried exploring Sterling Creek Forest. Why didn't she ask one of them?

When dad asked where I had gone, I told him I was at Linh's. I was lucky he didn't call her house and ask her mom. From now on, I would have to plan my trips to the forest carefully. It was funny how it was now easier to get into it thanks to the new opening the woman showed me yet a little more difficult to get out of the house. Dad would be suspicious if I kept saying I was going over to Linh's house. I would have to be careful with how long I spent in the forest and make sure my clothes weren't always dirty when I returned.

That night I was anxious to get back to the forest but knew I had to give it a couple of days. I had trouble falling asleep as I wondered what secret the woman had to tell me. I switched on my night lamp and got out of bed. I propped my pillows up, sat with a paper attached to a clipboard and began to write.

If you told me the words I put down on paper that night were going to change my life, I would have said you were crazy.

Chapter 11

Print Popularity

Okay, maybe the last thing I just said is not entirely true. The truth is, I wanted what I wrote to get me some attention. Well it did, starting on Tuesday after school. I waited until the other students left the newspaper club meeting. Mrs. Francine also headed out for a few minutes to do some photocopying in the office so it was just Derek and me.

"You said you wanted to show me something?" Derek asked, stapling some papers and placing them in one of the pockets of his binder.

"Yeah," I replied. "I wanted you to check this first and see if it's worth printing." I handed him a couple of sheets of paper that had a few folds at the top.

No more than a few seconds passed when his mouth dropped. His eyes widened and he had to sit down. He read a few more lines then looked up at me.

"Oh my... Dhanika, when... Were... Is this true?" Derek finally managed to ask.

"Yes. Do you think you can put it in the next Monthly?"

"Are you kidding!?" he practically shouted. "A giant newspaper like the Sterling Creek Chronicle would kill for something like this! And to think it'll be in our little school paper!"

"So, you'll print it?" I asked.

He stood up and walked towards the window and back.

"This'll look so good on my resumé. And what luck! Just before I start high school! It'll be good for you too!"

"Yes but will you print it?"

He looked confused. "Print what? Oh, the article! Yes, yes. Of course! Students who don't even go to this school will want it! Dhanika, you gave the Meadow Monthly such a huge boost. You're awesome!" He threw his arms around me.

"Thanks," I said, half pushing him away. "You said to come up with something interesting. Nothing's better than a true story everyone will want to read."

"For sure," agreed Derek. He looked at the papers again. "I'm going to re-type this and then run it by you tomorrow before we print the Monthly."

"Okay."

He was so excited he ran out of the room leaving his binder and backpack on the table. I shook my head, picked them up and headed after him down the hall.

Derek left most of what I had written untouched. He must have kept the other newspaper club members from seeing it until the last moment because none of them said much. They assumed that this May edition of the Meadow Monthly was going to be just as it had been over the past few months—an okay newspaper with some fun stuff. Nothing could have been further from what they thought.

It was Thursday around noon. I closed my locker and walked towards the lunchroom. There were loud voices and laughter that grew louder the closer I got. People rushed by me in pairs or threes with excitement waving copies of the Monthly. I turned the corner and there was the biggest crowd of kids in front of the lunchroom and the long table. Some were pushing to try and get their own copies. A few teachers were barking instructions trying to organize some straight lines for those who wanted the newspaper. Another teacher was trying to get the students out of the foyer and into the lunchroom. A girl in my science class jumped right in front of me. I stepped back startled.

"Oh my gosh! Dhanika, did you write this?" she exclaimed, showing a mouthful of metal braces.

"Yeah," I said. "But I didn't think it'd be..."

"That's so cool!" she continued. "What's going to happen now? Are you going to write something like this again next month? What made you decide to even...?"

This girl was like one of those toy robots that just had fresh batteries put in. Would her eyes and ears start flashing or lighting up? I excused myself and managed to get my own copy from one of the newspaper club members sitting at the table. I unfolded it and began to read the front page:

SPRING MEADOW STUDENT ENTERS STERLING CREEK!
Girl Warns of Secrets in Forbidden Forest

Have you ever wondered what it is really like in Sterling Creek Forest? Of course you have! Last week, I was able to speak to a girl who goes to this school about what it was like to walk among the trees and shrubbery that are off limits to kids. Her words will amaze you. The forest is not what you think.

The girl asked me not to use her real name, so we will just call her R. R is a normal, quiet girl who loves animals and orange freezies with the top cut off in a U-shape. She told me that she found a way to get under the big fence and has visited the forest "a couple of times. It's pretty quiet and peaceful there," she said. This is important information because kids were led to believe that it's an evil and dangerous place. R went on to say that, like other forests, this one has different animals. She said, "I saw rabbits, chipmunks and squirrels. Nothing scary."

You should know that R never visited the forest at night, so there's still a chance that scary monsters and ghosts come out then. R had no comment when I asked her if she planned to visit Sterling Creek Forest when the sky was dark and there was a full moon. She did say, for the record, that she didn't believe in ghosts.

What R wants all of the students at this school to know is that there's something else in the forest. A big, deep secret that has to do with the kids here and at other schools and neighbourhoods in Sterling Creek. The Meadow Monthly will print details about this secret in next month's final edition.

Keep reading the Monthly!

Written by Dhanika Adhikari (Grade 7)

As I folded the newspaper, I couldn't help feeling so proud. The Monthly was selling like crazy because of me. I was getting noticed by students and I had not even gone into the lunchroom yet. It was as though I were more important than the principal, maybe even the prime minister at that moment. Warm waves of happiness were swirling around inside me. A silly thought came to mind. *Maybe I could breathe into a bottle and trap these nice feelings and then let them out whenever I was sad.* I just had to make sure I brushed my teeth or chewed a piece of gum. I didn't want to seal any nasty breath.

Derek stood up and cupped his hands to project his voice. "We're sold out of the Monthly for now!" he bellowed. "More copies are being printed and should be ready in about fifteen minutes, so you can come back then!"

Some students groaned with disappointment but most began shuffling into the lunchroom or headed off to different clubs or activities. I took a few steps in the lunchroom and was showered with more compliments, friendly questions and greetings.

"Great article, Dhanika! I was never interested in the

Monthly until now."

"Who's R? Are you BFFs?"

"I just bought three copies of the Monthly and I don't even know how to read!" joked a boy in Grade 6. He ran off laughing.

"Hey Dhanika."

I've heard this voice before, I thought, tracing the spot from where it was coming. It was that tall, pretty girl in Grade 8 with whom I exchanged words in the hallway not so long ago. She was sitting with three of her princess-like friends.

"Hi," I said nervously. *What's going on here?* I wondered.

Another one spoke. "Nice article." She finished applying lip gloss, snapped the compact shut and smacked her shiny lips together in a pout. "I didn't know you wrote so good, you know, with like words and stuff," she said.

"Thanks," I told her. I tightened up and waited for them to call me a loser or some other mean name. It didn't happen.

The first girl who spoke pulled out a chair. "Cool story. Come sit with us."

I sat with them and looked around at them cautiously as they talked, laughed and asked me about the article. As the lunch break went on, I became a bit more comfortable with these girls. Actually they were more like young women the way they carried on. I observed them as I ate. Their hair was straight with blonde or brown streaks. A couple of them had strands that swung in front of their eyes. The short sleeve tops they wore were pink, black or blue and white striped. Some of the tops gave up near the upper arms and didn't even bother to cover all of them. A touch of lotion made their shoulders shine as they threw their heads back and shook with laughter. *Wow,* I thought. *I can even smell how cool these girls are. I bet they never sweated a day in their lives!* I found out some names the longer I sat with them. The one who spoke first was Parveen. The others were Christy, Ramandeep and Mylah.

"So, what's it like to be famous?" asked Ramandeep, tapping her polished fingernails on the table.

"I don't feel famous," I replied. "Okay, well, maybe like a mini celebrity but that's it!" Everyone laughed.

"Dhanika, you're so funny!" Mylah said.

"Thanks," I replied.

They all stood up and adjusted their handbags. "Come walk back to homeroom with us," Parveen said with a smile.

I stood up and headed towards the lunchroom exit. It seemed as though everyone was in as good a mood as I was today. We walked by a table near a corner with the vending machines and I spotted Zoe, Sarah and Linh. For some reason, they gave me sad looks of disgust as I walked past them and headed out with my new friends. What was their problem? Why didn't they want to share this happy moment with me? I couldn't figure it out.

Chapter 12

Broken Friends and Locket Ends

Sometimes you can read a story, watch an entire TV show or online video and not remember a thing. The words, pictures and sounds come off the pages or screen but your mind is somewhere else to the point where nothing about the characters or storyline stays with you.

This was happening to me right now in French class. It was the second last period of the day and we were given a few paragraphs to read about Madeleine Desrochers's favourite animals and seasons. Another paragraph was about different types of 'musique.' There were sets of questions to answer afterward, including a fill-in-the-blanks section where we had to write the missing verb in each sentence. I plodded through the reading and wrote what I thought were the correct answers but my mind was so far away from Madeleine and 'avoir' and 'être.' It was as though my school brain had taken a vacation. I began drawing the letter 'S,' the tall kind with sharp corners along with little trees and hearts in my agenda.

The other part of my brain was going through all of the events that had taken place earlier in the day. I loved the attention and excitement my piece in the Monthly had given me. There is no feeling in the world like being noticed, liked and complimented. And even just sitting with Parveen and her friends, talking laughing and sharing the same air made me feel important. I even felt as pretty as all of those girls just by being near them. So why did Linh seem so annoyed? I looked over to her table group. Normally we exchanged silly faces during quiet work periods but she barely looked at me this afternoon. Maybe she was just tired or jealous. I decided to find out.

I reached into my desk and quietly ripped a corner off a sheet of lined paper. I removed a gel pen from my pencil case and wrote:

'U mad?'

I folded the paper three times. Prathanan, whose desk was connected to mine, gave me a strange look and continued with his work. I got up and walked towards the pencil sharpener. Brushing the side of Linh's desk, I swiftly dropped the tiny note on Linh's open binder so that it would blend in with the whiteness of her paper. After giving the sharpener's handle a few weak turns, I returned to my desk and waited.

Linh quietly got up, walked to the grey recycling bin and ripped the paper into pieces. It fell like thick snowflakes. She snatched two pieces that ended up on the floor, tossed them in and went back to her seat.

What's going on? She always replies to my notes! Why doesn't she want to be my...

"Dhanika, ne passez pas des notes!" Madame Dupont sang out.

Shoot! I thought. *I'm slipping in my passing skills. I need to remember to practise. Maybe I'll write myself a note...*

Probably not a good idea, right?

The classroom phone rang. Madame Dupont answered it, looked at me, then switched languages.

"Dhanika, could you go back to your homeroom now? Mr. Stellick would like to speak to you."

As I got up and headed for the door, I felt the stares and whispers of "What'd she do?" "Is she in trouble?" I began to sweat a little as I walked down the hall, turned the corner and entered my homeroom. Mr. Stellick was seated at his desk. Beside him was Mrs. Sharma, the guidance counsellor.

Oh boy. Two teachers for the price of one. I stood near the doorway.

"Come in and have a seat, Dhanika," instructed Mr. Stellick. I sat down in one of the chairs near his desk.

Mrs. Sharma held up a copy of the Monthly and got right to the point. "Dhanika, this article you wrote is very serious. Not only for you but for the person to whom you spoke."

I bit my bottom lip and twisted my right foot so hard I was sure it left a smudge on the floor underneath.

She continued. "Who's the student? What grade is she in?"

Trapped! What should I say? Hmm... Maybe I'll tell them that this girl's English isn't very good. Yes, that's it! She and I made up a language called Ooba Jooba that only the two of us speak and understand... No, they're too smart for that!

How about *'I'd like to tell you, but the girl I spoke to moved to Pakistan...?' Nope. They'd ask me more questions and nail me for sure!*

"Dhanika?" asked Mr. Stellick.

Think!

"I've never met her," I finally blurted out. "She must have found out from someone that I help with the Monthly and called me last night. Our call display had 'unknown number' on it when it rang. She told me about her time in the forest without telling me her name and I wrote down as much as I could."

I could feel my body heating up from the lies that just came out of my mouth. If I had been a wooden puppet, my nose would've been touching the chalkboard from where I was sitting. The two teachers looked at each other. Then Mrs. Sharma spoke.

"If what you wrote is true, there are lots of problems

here. First, this girl is breaking the law by going into the forest. Second, there's a safety issue. Who knows what might happen to her if she goes back in?"

"And if something happened to this girl and the teachers and principals knew about her visits to the forest, we'll be in hot water," added Mr. Stellick, waving his index finger between him and Mrs. Sharma.

I nodded. "I don't know her name," I quietly reminded them.

Mrs. Sharma wrote a few notes and then looked up at me. "Okay," she said. "We've documented our little talk we just had and your teacher and I will keep copies in our files. If you have any information about who this girl is, you've got to let us know."

"Okay. I will."

"Great. Thanks, Dhanika," said Mr. Stellick.

I walked out of the room, praying they would not call me in again. The smudge was still on the floor along with, I was sure, some drops of nervous sweat on the seat.

The new entrance into the forest that the woman in the cabin showed me was much better than squeezing under the fence. I decided to visit her after school that day when the Meadow Monthly had come out and all the excitement happened. I was able to get in the forest through a large drainage tunnel that ran from a part where a bridge on the main street sloped. This tunnel led all the way to a dirt path. I just had to make sure nobody saw me ducking into the bushes from the sidewalk. I then had to walk down another dirt path which led to an opening in the forest. Once I was in, I remembered the way over to the river I had to cross. Thankfully my backpack was light today and I had no math textbook to carry. Free hands were important in case I had to act quickly.

Even though the woman told me these parts weren't patrolled, I kept looking around in case police officers or guards decided to jump out and drag me off to jail. I wish I didn't have to worry about getting caught. It would have been nicer to just walk into the forest, enjoy its sounds, sights and smells and walk around like a regular person. I was always tense when I entered and left. It was weird that the only place where I felt safe was a stranger's house hidden among the trees.

Walking through the forest gave me time to think about all that had happened that day. I didn't have too much time to wonder about the nice things students had told me when the Monthly came out and the time I spent during lunch sitting with Parveen and the older girls. Some people would call them popular but I think of them differently. Popular girls are ones who have many friends and others wish they were friends with them. They seem to be busy socializing during and after school. Nothing seems to be wrong with them. Of course, they are not perfect but they're pretty close to it. I wouldn't say Parveen and her friends were popular, they're just cool. Cool people don't care how many friends they have. They don't follow anyone and have a style of their own—probably an expensive style. Not only are they cool, they know they're cool and nobody can stop them.

And to think they wanted to be friends with me! I never had any cool, pretty friends. Could I be friends with these girls? I didn't see why not. I was disappointed that Linh, Zoe and Sarah wouldn't sit with me at lunch today and Linh didn't even respond to my note in French. Why was she being mean? I would sit with new friends of hers. I even put up with her weird buddy Zoe. Why isn't she doing the same for me? I decided to find out the next day from Sarah what was bothering Linh. It couldn't be my fault, I was sure of that.

As I got closer to the cabin, I could sense something was wrong. It was way too quiet, even for Sterling Creek Forest. I knocked a few times and when there was no answer, I pushed the door open.

"Hello?" I called out. "Are you home?"

I stepped in and walked around. Everything seemed to be in place as it was the first time I visited. I noticed there were some apples, oranges and bananas on one of the tables as well as a few creased plastic bags with the grocery store logo. I walked towards the corner where the chairs were. Maybe she had fallen asleep. There was no one. I sat and waited.

My eyes travelled to the wooden shelves that had jars, bottles and boxes of what looked like crackers. On the right side, I could see different kinds of bead necklaces and chains. One of them was shiny and, almost immediately, a tiny glint caught my eye. It seemed to be a thin gold chain with a pendant on the bottom.

I froze, refusing to believe my eyes.

Seven letters...

The pendant was made with seven letters!

MO, A, DAUG...

"Dhanika?" came a voice from the doorway. "Are you in here? I have missed you."

Still stunned by the pendant, I said the first thing that came to mind:

"Mom?"

Chapter 13

Maximillian Sturgess

The woman looked at me. Her wide eyes and slightly raised eyebrow were a combination of surprise and confusion. "Mom?" she repeated softly. "What do you mean?"

I felt mixed up inside. My feelings of excitement and fear seemed to be riding the same see-saw. I could hear the air going in and out of my lungs in short spurts as though it were being controlled by a bike pump.

"It's you mom, right? It has to be!" I whispered.

"I don't understand," the woman replied. She walked inside, set a few soiled things down on the table and wiped her hands on a pink towel. She motioned for me to sit down and pulled up a chair.

"You think I'm your mother?"

I nodded as my eyes began to well up with tears. I brushed them away.

The woman put a hand on my knee. "Why do you think that?"

I didn't know where to begin. I tried to speak but everything came spilling out in a stuttering mess.

"I, I... have this pendant. It's this... It's... She gave it to me a long time ago." I removed it from under my shirt to show her. "I was little but remember that she kept the other half."

I pointed to the beads nearby. "You, you... have it... that one with the other letters and when you bring... put them all at... together, they spell 'mother and daughter.'"

The woman walked over to the pendant and chain. She examined it for a moment and then returned to me.

"I'm so sorry, Dhanika. Really, I am. But I'm not your mother."

What? No! Why are you saying this? I could feel steel nails poking my stomach as though someone were in a hurry to finish redecorating. "You have to be!" I exclaimed. "Our pendants fit, you're nice to me and, I... I... haven't seen her for so long..." I was out of words. I buried my face in my lap, crying softly and rocking back and forth.

She patted me on the back. "I won't pretend to know how much you miss your mother. And I wish I could tell you I'm her but I'm not. I'm not going to sit here and lie to you."

I looked up at her. My face must have been a mess because the woman stepped away for a moment and returned with a large piece of paper towel. I rubbed my face with it twice.

"What about the pendant? Where'd you get it?" I asked.

"Someone left it in the picnic area by the community centre and never came back for it," she replied.

"But I thought my mom and I were the only ones in the world who have it."

She shook her head. "I don't mean to sound rude but you can get pendants like this in most department or jewellery stores."

Suddenly, the most precious thing I owned did not seem special at all. Millions of moms and daughters probably had them. My face went from sadness to a scowl. I felt like pulling it off my neck and flinging it across the room. The woman noticed my changed mood.

"That doesn't mean your pendant still isn't special," she

reminded me.

"It's not special if so many other people have it. I thought I was the only one!"

"It doesn't matter where the pendant came from," she said. "What matters is someone who loves you gave you something because she wanted you to have a part of her with you. It's not the gift itself, it's about how it makes you and the other person feel."

I never thought of it that way. I was far from cheerful but sat back and let her words sink in. Finally, I spoke.

"Okay. I get that you're not my mom. So, who are you? I don't even know what to call you. What's your name?"

"Jinan," she said.

Nice, I thought.

"How did you end up living in this forest? Why not just live in a regular house like normal people?"

"I'm normal," Jinan reminded me. "I think so-called 'normal people' do very strange things that other normal people don't bother to look at and try to change because they're afraid of not being normal. Do you follow what I'm saying?"

"No," I told her. "I don't get it."

"Okay," she said, starting over. "I used to live in a regular house in a neighbourhood not too far from Sterling Creek a few years ago with my fiancé. Everything seemed to be going well. I worked and so did he and we had a good life. The problem was we had too much and used more than we needed. I got tired of it. Plus, he wasn't as nice as he used to be. He became very difficult to live with."

"What do you mean 'had too much?'" I asked.

"Everybody's so wasteful around here," Jinan said, spreading her arms wide. "They create so much garbage, eat bad things and throw away stuff that still works just so they can get something new. Then they throw those things out and replace them. Look at all the items in here." She pointed across the room. "These are all things people have thrown out. I'm trying to live what I believe."

"What's that?"

"I believe we can be less wasteful, use the land more and replace what we take from it. And nobody else seems to be interested in living that way but I decided to do it."

I nodded. *Talk about a real-life example of save the trees,* I thought. At school, I read about pollution's effect on the environment and how we can live healthier, greener lives but never actually met someone who changed her life because she felt it was the right thing to do. Jinan gave up a good life to live with nature but wasn't it so lonely being out here by herself? I know she spoke about being near people who used the community centre but that doesn't replace friends and family! She also spoke about "secrets" of the forest and I was going to find out right now what she meant.

"The last time we met, you said this forest has secrets. Is it you? Are you the secret who lives hidden away in the forest?"

She shook her head. "It's more important than I am. I'm just one living thing in here. Sooner or later, I'll have to find another place to live. The problem is a lie the grown-ups of Sterling Creek have been telling the children."

"What lie?"

"This forest doesn't have dangerous snakes, scary monsters or evil dogs. These are just things the adults say to keep the children out of the forest and from finding out."

"Finding out what?" I asked.

"What's really hidden in this forest," said Jinan. She walked over to the table and held up a dirty plate. "This is what some adults in Sterling Creek don't want anyone to find."

My eyes widened. "That's it?" I asked surprised. "That's the big secret? A dirty dish?" *Just use soap and a sponge!* I thought.

She smiled as she walked back to where I was sitting. "This is more valuable than most people realize. It's an antique silver plate from the late 17th or early 18th century. Long before Sterling Creek developed into the community you and I know, there were farming families who settled on this land. One of those families was headed by Maximillian Sturgess. The Sturgess family was hard-working and proud. They established and maintained several traditions, one of which was preserving important family heirlooms."

"What are heirlooms?" I asked.

"Different objects that are special. They are passed down from one generation to the next," replied Jinan. She continued.

"Mr. Sturgess polished and restored several pieces of cutlery and ornaments that he had brought with him from Ireland. He was ready to pass them on to his four children—two sons and two daughters—but tragedy struck. One afternoon, the Sturgess children were playing in the river when strong currents swept them away. They struggled, fought and cried for help but it was no use. They drowned and were found hours later motionless on top of several jagged rocks with cuts and bruises. Mr. and Mrs. Sturgess were devastated. It was as though part of them died that day with their children. They tried a few times to have more children but failed. Unwilling to betray the love he had for his children, Maximillian refused to bestow the treasured cutlery and artifacts upon anyone else. He returned to the land near the river and buried the objects in several places. Perhaps the roaming souls of his offspring could enjoy them in whatever realm they resided." Jinan paused.

"There are still other things out there," she said, pointing toward the leaves and trees through the window. "Plates, spoons, gold and silver coins and other stuff. A whole treasure trove that has already been discovered!"

"Discovered by whom?" I asked.

"A few people. People who work for the government know about it. So do some police officers and the owner of the Sterling Creek Heritage Department. Why do you think they put up a fence and sign trying to keep children out? They're scared that some young person is going to stumble on the hidden treasure that they keep for themselves!"

"They keep it for themselves? How do you know?"

"I see and hear them digging at night. They take turns and come in small groups with flashlights. These men put whatever they find in a large sack and haul it away. But this isn't a 'finders keepers' game we're talking about here. The law says you have to report any archaeological finds to the federal government. You have to be honest and these guys aren't!"

I looked at the dirty plate and then studied the window and floor. Was this woman lying? What did any of this have to do with me? Why didn't she get someone else to help? Someone taller, maybe older...

"That's quite a history lesson about the Sturgess family. I didn't know about them. But why did you choose me to..."

"Save the day?" she interrupted, finishing my question. "Changes can start with anyone. Look at how I made my life different by coming out here to live. I'm a lot older than you, though. Change starts with young people. They're curious, smart and full of energy. There are far too many adults who are afraid to change their habits and embrace other ways of thinking. They'd rather keep things the way they are. But you're not like that. You're young, smart and open to new ideas. And it took a lot of bravery to find me in this forest...

"Uh, I kind of found you by accident," I reminded her.

"That's okay," Jinan said. "You were meant to find me. The forest brought you here. And you'll be the one who stops these evil people from stealing."

Me? How could I be a hero? How could I go up against bad guys and enemies? I couldn't even be a good friend at school! Maybe I needed training, super powers or a big bag of tricks.

"I don't know if I can do it. This is a big deal," I said.

"It's not something I get asked to do every day!"

"You'll be fine," she told me. "Come. Let me show you some spots where they dig." She took me by the arm.

We left the cabin and I cautiously followed her up the ravine, still unsure if I would be able to stand up to a bunch of thieves in the night who were braver and stronger than I.

Chapter 14

A Song for Troubled Times

Jinan and I visited different clearings and small hills that afternoon. She remembered the locations of each place that had been dug up by marking nearby trees. The mayor and his group of thieves did a really good job of covering their tracks. There were no strange arrangements of rocks and branches that could have been a sign that a group had set up their tools, equipment and once in a while, a small fire to keep warm. They erased their tracks and other clues that showed someone had been digging. If a person happened to be taking a stroll during the day in this forest, that person would never guess that he or she were walking on or beside buried treasures.

Jinan spoke about coming up with a plan to get proof that the mayor and his group were digging up and keeping objects and artifacts. I never did anything like this in my life. The only times I could remember having to prove something were those problem-solving math questions where you were asked to do that dumb nonsense like "justify your answer." Why? Math is math. You're either right or wrong! Another time was during a mock election in our Grade 5 class during our government unit in social studies. We had a debate and I had to prove that the other political party's idea of not having students line up in front of the classroom in the hallway would be chaotic. I never really understood why you had to prove certain things. There is stuff everyone knows. Why can't they just accept it?

The treasure in Sterling Creek Forest was a different issue altogether. This wasn't a school assignment or homework that was going to get marked. It was something that the community needed to know and telling or begging them to believe me would not work. It would be difficult to prove that people everyone thought were the good guys were doing bad things. People who held important jobs and others who kept things quiet and well hidden...

Wait a minute. Have they really been doing this? Forget about justifying an answer. I needed proof! Jinan was pretty smart and I liked her for being so nice to me. She also made me feel special by giving me the responsibility of taking on these bad people to make the forest a place for young people but I needed to know more.

"I'm not so sure about some of the stuff you told me," I said, brushing aside some leaves that tickled my cheek.

"You don't believe me or you don't trust me?" Jinan asked.

"Both. I'm a bit scared. What if this is just a trick and I end up getting hurt? I'm just a kid!"

To my surprise she replied, "No you're not. You're a girl."

"What?"

She reached in her backpack and pulled out a spade. "A kid is a baby goat. You don't have horns and a tail." Jinan smiled. "Unless there's something you're hiding from me."

"A kid means baby goat?"

"Yes," she said, bending her knees and jabbing the soil. "Look it up in the dictionary. It's true."

Normally I would have laughed at her joke about me having the features of a goat but I remained serious, thinking about what the two of us were doing. I didn't want to die trying to stop a bunch of grownups!

Jinan continued to dig with her back to me. I was about to tell her again how worried I was when I felt something warm and sweet near my cheeks and nose. At first, I thought it was the petals of a flower but slowly realized it was no plant. It was singing. The words floated around my face, filling my head with a warm, soothing feeling:

When the last ray of sun goes down
And the cold and dark are all around
Don't fear, cry or shake
Warm in my arms you'll be
When you awake.

She stood up and looked at me with one of her warm smiles. Now I had even more questions.

"Was that you singing?"

"Yes."

"Wow. I thought it was coming from somewhere else! That was really nice! I had no idea you could sing like that," I said. "Where'd you learn that song?"

"I just made it up," she told me. "I used to sing it to some of the young children I used to babysit when I was a teenager. Other times, I sing it out here when I'm among the trees. I guess it just stuck with me."

I really couldn't say how I was feeling at that moment. Music can do that to a person. There are songs I love as much as the one Jinan sang. But it is hard to say why. Sometimes feelings can't be turned into words.

"I really liked that," I said.

"Thanks," she replied. She held up a couple of dirty coins. "Here's some more stuff. I'll add it to the plates I have back at the cabin." I took a quick look at them while she cleaned off the spade and put it in her backpack.

"You still don't believe me about what's going on in the forest, do you?" she asked.

It was like she could read my mind. I handed her the coins. "Sort of," I said. "I need to see something to believe it."

"Okay," Jinan said. "I've figured out that these thieves come out on Monday and Friday nights. Today is Thursday. So here's the plan. Come back tomorrow night around 10:30. Those men usually end up in the forest around 11:00. Then you'll see for yourself what they do."

"That's scary," I said, knowing that these guys would be in the forest listening for sounds and people spying on them.

She touched my arm. "Don't worry. I'll show you where you and I will meet. Just make sure you bring a small flashlight and camera. Can you do that?" she asked.

"Yeah," I replied, remembering the pink digital camera in my top drawer and mini flashlight on my desk.

"Good! I won't keep you out too long and before you know it, we'll nail them and the forest will be a different place, thanks to you!"

"Okay," I said. I still wasn't thrilled about the idea of coming back to the forest when it was dark but started to feel a little better about it.

Jinan showed me our meeting place and wished me luck. "I'll see you tomorrow night" were her last words before she slipped away into the bushes. I headed up towards the tunnel that led to the street.

I know I mentioned before that Fridays were an easy-going day at Sunny Meadow but this Friday was tough. I got caught twice by teachers for not paying attention during class when we were taking up some homework questions. My mind was not only set on building up courage to face what lay ahead in Sterling Creek Forest that night but also being brave enough to face Linh. We barely spoke to each other at our locker since the Monthly came out and I still wanted to know why she was being so mean. I spotted Sarah going down the stairs towards the library later that morning. I was heading that way, so I caught up with her.

"Hey," I said. "Wait up!"

She gave me a sideways glance and said nothing. We continued down the hall.

"How've you been?" I asked.

"What do you care?" Sarah replied sharply.

"I care," I said. "Why are you being so mean?"

She stopped near the stairwell. "I'm being mean? How can you say that when you're the one who ignores us?"

"Ignore you? I'm still the same. I have some new friends and I don't see why..."

"Ever since you wrote that article and became Miss Popular Writer you think you're so cool," Sarah reminded me.

"No, I don't," I said, becoming angry. "What do you want me to do if people like it and want to talk to me?"

"You shouldn't forget who your real friends are, that's all," she said, opening the door.

I was about to say something else but didn't bother. Sarah was already walking down the stairs and I had to keep going.

The beige metal library door was open when I arrived. I scanned the tables and spotted Linh sitting with her back to me. I walked over and sat down in the chair across from her.

"Did I do something wrong?" I asked.

She said nothing. I decided to remind her about my efforts from not so long ago.

"What do I have to do?" I asked, throwing my hands up. "I've tried talking and writing you notes. I don't know what to..."

"Nothing," Linh replied with a tired voice. "You don't have to do anything."

I was confused. "What do you mean?"

"You already showed you'd rather be friends with those girls in Grade 8 who think they're better than..."

"Hey, they're nice," I said. "If you gave them a chance..."

"Nice?" Linh's eyes widened. She raised her voice. "They're the same girls who called you names the first week you were at this school! And now you want to be friends with them?"

The librarian interrupted. "Ladies, you're here to study quietly. You know that. Drop the volume or find another place to work," she sternly warned.

We bowed our heads and feigned studying. I pretended to work on an editing and revising exercise as I lowered my voice. "What's wrong with having another group of friends?" I asked Linh.

"Nothing!" she whispered back. "But don't sit here and tell me that those fake, wannabe princesses are really your friends because they're not!"

'Remember your friends.' Not too long ago, Joss told me this. Who were my friends right now? It was almost impossible to figure out. I blurted out, "Yeah? What made you the friend expert?"

Linh shook her head. "Everyone sees it except you. Think about it. You only became friends after the article came out. Before that, they didn't want anything to do with you!"

"You could've sat with us at lunch," I told her. "Why didn't you just come over instead of sitting away from me and my friends thinking that those girls were bad?"

"I don't need to sit with them to know what they're like! They don't talk to any regular people unless they wear expensive stuff and talk a certain way. Those girls don't want to be friends with anyone who's not like them."

Without thinking, I spat out, "You're just jealous."

Linh stood up. "Think whatever you want but you and I made a promise to keep that stuff in the forest a secret between us. And I can count one person sitting here who didn't keep it to herself." She pointed down on the wooden table with her index finger. "If you look deep enough inside, Dhanika, you know I'm right. I don't feel like being friends with someone who forgets about people who are real friends and actually nice to you." She grabbed her books and binder and left.

I stared at the bookshelves and the clock on the wall. It was hard to believe that in just twenty-four hours, I went from getting so much attention and having friends to being disliked by Linh and Sarah—two people I knew truly cared about me even before I wrote the article. On top of everything I had to remember for tonight's encounter in the forest, the problem with my two friends weighed down on my shoulders, giving me yet another thing to worry about. What could I do? I needed help and had just lost two people who may have been able to give some good advice or just be there to share a freezie or a laugh. I got up and exited the library, hoping I had enough brain power and strength to be able to figure things out on my own.

Chapter 15

Chains and Other Challenges

I don't know about you but whenever I am in a hurry, I always end up having a million things to do. And something annoying always seems to come up and slow me down. Friday night came as quickly as I thought it would but it seemed to take dad forever to turn off the kitchen and living room lights and head upstairs. I told him about an hour ago that I was going to bed early, so my bedroom light was already off. When he finally made it up, I heard sounds from the TV and worried that he would never go to sleep. I had my room door open a crack and nervously tapped my foot on the carpet. As soon as I saw the strip of light under his door turn black, I checked my alarm clock. 10:20! I was going to have to be the world's quietest tornado as I rushed to get out of the house.

I slipped out the back door, remembering to take my key, flashlight and camera. I also had a clipboard with some paper and a pen. They were safe inside the backpack that was swung over my shoulders. I took my bike out of the garage earlier and it leaned it against the side of the house. The last thing I needed was the sound of the garage screeching and rattling at this hour.

There was a slight chill in the air. The streetlights lit up the pavement and grass on the patches of lawn I rode past.

Occasionally, I would hear the soft cries of bats overhead and the slight rustle of trees. So far, it was a smooth ride and calmness settled in. I had done this before, right? Nothing could stop me. Everything was going as planned until the Hatchford decided to toss a challenge my way.

At first, I thought it was some stray cat or hungry dog when I heard a short groaning sound. Suddenly, I couldn't feel any resistance as I pedalled. It was as though I were on one of those exercise bikes in someone's basement or the gym. I pushed down and moved my legs. The pedals spun faster but the bike was slowing down. I twisted the handlebars left and right as I tried to control the bike. Finally, I just squeezed the brake grips and came to a sudden, shaky stop. I almost knocked over a couple of potted plants that were on the edge of someone's lawn.

I wheeled my bike away from the grass, put the kickstand in place and bent down to have a look. The chain had come off its gears and was swinging like a skipping rope. Immediately, the silly skipping song I used to sing in Grade 3 filled my head and refused to leave. I don't know why. The timing could not have been any worse:

Strawberry shortcake
Appleberry pie
Who's gonna be your lucky guy?
Is it A, B, C...?

I'll take any guy! I thought. *I don't care. As long as he knows how to fix this oily chain!*

I shook my head and tilted it, hoping the song would leak out of my ear and leave me alone. I had to concentrate. No lucky guy was coming tonight and I had less than ten minutes to get to Sterling Creek Forest. I was on my own.

I took out my flashlight and shone it on the chain. It was loose and ropey but I could tell that one way or another it had to be put back on the gears. I lifted my bike by the seat at a 30-degree angle and kept it in place with one hand. I glanced at the chain to see which parts weren't gripping the gear's teeth. Reaching with my other hand, I pulled the greasy chain over the big gear first, then the smaller gear at the back. Nothing. It swung back and forth like a shaky bridge. I wiped some sweat off my forehead and placed the bike down. I lifted it and started again. This time I gave the chain a quick jerk before laying it on the gears. I heard a click. Was it okay? I turned the pedal with my smudged hand. It moved without any crazy spinning or strange sounds. I did it! Nice! I mounted and raced down the street towards the community centre.

I inched down the small dirt hill from the main road, which was a tricky thing to do while gripping handlebars. I almost tumbled to the bottom and skidded to a stop right against the front tire of my bike. I felt rubber and spokes force their way right up against me. Luckily, I was wearing long pants or I would've ended up with the tattoo of a tic tac toe board on my shin. I stood my bike up. Now all that was left to do was get through the drainage tunnel.

I don't even have a colour or description of how dark it was, so just to give you an idea, cover one of your eyes with a tight hand. That's the kind of darkness which lay in front of me. There was a faint light at the end but who knows what scary stuff was ready to attack me on the inside? I took out my flashlight and turned it on. A yellowish, white pole shot out in front of me.

I crept slowly through the tunnel, shining the light in front of me and near the ceiling of the tunnel. I managed to scare some bugs and mice but so far, no werewolves or hungry dogs were crouching ready to pounce. I shone the light behind me a few times to make sure I wasn't being followed. The more steps I took, the less afraid I became. As I drew nearer to the end, I could see the outline of some bushes and trees thanks to the weak light coming from the lamppost in the distance. I shone the light behind me one more time just in case some napping creature decided to wake up hungry. There was nothing behind me. I quickly turned the flashlight to the centre of my body and was about to switch it off when I noticed something odd. The light seemed to be reflecting off something. How? I was right by the tunnel's exit and close to the light from the lamppost. I squinted and jumped back. My heart leaped to my throat and stayed there for a few seconds before returning to my chest. The flashlight caught the glassy, cold eyes of something. I moved closer and saw something shaggy with sharp fur. I could hear a weird gurgling noise coming from its throat. Suddenly, two other hairy friends decided to join the creature. They all stared at me, twitching their whiskers with fake innocence, ready to pounce like an unfair three-against-one wrestling match. I could hear their nail-like claws digging into the dirt. *This is really bad*, I thought to myself. I don't think there was one body part of mine that wasn't quivering with fear because I now realized what I was up against. The fact that they travelled together and looked around to try and cause trouble meant these creatures in front of the tunnel could be only one thing.

Raccoons.

They paced back and forth waiting for me to make a move. Should I shut my eyes and try to jump past them? Bad idea. That would excite them and they would chase me. And I wasn't about to turn back and run in a dark tunnel with these nasty fur faces behind me. At least here I could see what they were about to do. *How about I wait until they leave? No, silly. You're already late for Jinan and maybe even the treasure robbers.* I looked around where I stood to see if there was anything I could use. Small plants and some leafy weeds were no good. I could feel the raccoons staring me up and down deciding which part of me they would each devour.

Wait a minute. Devour. That's it!

I reached into my backpack and pulled out a brown paper bag that had my leftover lunch. *This might work,* I thought, slowly walking towards the group. Their heads immediately turned to me.

I flung half a turkey sandwich near one of the bushes behind them. Two of them quickly darted back towards the sound it made as it landed. They began grunting and body checking each other trying to get the largest pieces. The third one—the one that first appeared by himself a couple of minutes ago—stayed where he was. 'You better have something better than that,' he seemed to say.

I didn't have time to think. Before he could attack, I slid him a brownish, yellow apple which wobbled to a stop by one of his hind legs. He turned to look at what had just hit him and then looked back at me. A clump of aluminum foil was all I had left. Luckily it contained a piece of vanilla cake. I tossed it right at him.

I don't know if it was the smell of the vanilla or the rough, pointy foil but he turned his attention away from me and began biting and tearing away at it. I wasted no time. There was nothing in front of the dirt path now, so I ran for it. I quickly looked back to check on those crazy mammals. The two raccoon buddies were still hitting each other and trying to pry bread crusts from each other. The first raccoon's face was covered in so much white icing, I thought he was shaving. *I hope you cut your face on the foil, you furry dope!* I know it's not a nice thing to think but I didn't have time to sit with them in a circle and try to make friends with them!

I slowed down, then dropped to my knees in front of a large rock. I put my hands out in front on the cool, hard soil panting. Just then, I felt a hand on my shoulder. I nearly jumped out of my pants! I scrambled back and dug my heels in the ground doing a backwards crab walk.

"It's okay, Dhanika," a soft voice spoke. "It's me. Are you okay? What kept you?"

"Yeah, I'm fine." Through gasps and coughs I told her everything that happened that evening.

"Thank goodness you're okay!" she said.

From my backpack, I removed a water bottle and took a long sip. I then turned it over on each of my hands to rub off the grease from my bike. Most of it disappeared. Jinan handed me a soft cloth and I wiped my hands and face. I started feeling better as she reviewed our plan.

She said, "They're going to be here soon. There could be two of them or four or five and my guess is they're going to finish digging up this area." She waved her hand towards the clearing in front of us.

"I'm going to be on the high part up there moving between the trees and taking some pictures. "Did you bring the camera?"

I reached into my backpack and handed it to her.

"Thanks. Stay low right here behind these bushes. They won't be able to see you, especially if you're really still. Wait here until I get back."

"Okay," I said.

I knelt down on my knees and waited. The forest air had become cooler. Even the leaves and trees were shuddering this spring night. I took out my clipboard and with the help of the thin moonlight began to draw different shapes and faces. I wasn't sure how much time passed. It felt like a couple of hours. I let out a quiet yawn and inhaled the leafy aromas and the gingery smell of the surrounding flowers. Some mosquitoes hummed near my ears and I quietly swatted them away.

A new smell began to float towards my hiding spot. It was the sharp scent of cigarette smoke mixed with musky cologne. I could hear deep, muffled voices, laughing and words that would have made my cluster of four students in social studies class lose group points. As they entered the clearing, I could make out four large, shadowy figures. Soon, the sound of pickaxes and shovels hitting the dirt joined forces with their smells and took over this part of the forest. I inched down as far as I could on my stomach and watched. In the distance, a series of flashes went off. A couple of times the men looked up but were unable to locate it. They called out and walked around the clearing but saw nothing and returned to their work.

A large disc went sailing through the air and landed a few feet in front of me. A few minutes later, long cylinders and flat time pieces followed as well as sounds that reminded me of someone dropping loose change and marbles on the floor. The treasure was piling up right in front of me!

I reached for my pen and began writing everything I could see. Together with Jinan's pictures we would have proof about what was going on in the forest at night.

Suddenly I heard a noise as if someone were in pain. At first I thought it was me. I could hear the sound of feet and legs on the ground and thought that the men had gotten into a fight. I parted some of the bushes to get a better look.

One of the men grunted and said, "Let's split. I don't want to get attacked by some animal. We got what we need!"

"Hold on, hold on," said another. "Wait for those other two to get back. I think they found some more stuff!"

The two of them walked towards where I was hiding. I held my breath and prayed. I heard the clanging of metal as they dropped everything into a sack and began dragging it on the ground. Good. They had not seen me. I listened as they began refilling the holes they had dug. Then I heard other voices entering the clearing. Some animal or something was with them and wasn't walking on its own. It sounded as though it was being dragged or forced to walk. *Raccoons?* I wondered. I parted the bushes.

I couldn't believe it. Jinan was a crumpled mess lying on

her side in the clearing at the feet of one of the men who spoke:

"You bag the stuff?" he asked.

"Yeah," replied another.

"Good," he said. "We're takin' this with us too." He dragged Jinan across the clearing and the five of them disappeared among the black trees.

Chapter 16

Solitary Travail

The forest never seemed so dark and lonely. I stood up and leaned against a tree whose bark I could barely feel against my back. Numbness had taken over and removed all of the senses from my body. My eyes produced no tears and my brain could not make me feel afraid or worried. All I was able to do at this point was breathe.

With shaking hands, I picked up my clipboard and backpack and managed to swing one strap over my shoulder. I walked across the clearing where the men had just dug. They were careful not to leave the earth perfectly smooth. Some of it was still clumped and uneven to camouflage any sign of recent digging. I headed toward the trees on the small cliff where Jinan was hiding to see if they changed their minds and left her in some bushes around there. I switched on my flashlight without even thinking that one of the men could have decided to come back and look for something else. Sterling Creek Forest had thrown so much at me tonight and other times before, it was as though I had been through some kind of torture test. I had survived so much I felt like I stepped out of my body and was watching some other version of me move through the forest. I just didn't care anymore if some new animal came out from behind the trees or I got hurt in some way.

"Jinan!" I whispered as I walked along the cliff between the trees. "You there?"

Some leaves and branches rustled and swayed but no answer came. I had no plan to follow and was trying to do the impossible task of visiting every spot where she could have been. Everything looked the same. It was hopeless. Those awful men had taken her away and here I was in a dark forest that, on the one hand, showed me some secrets yet had no answers about my friend. I turned to head home, when I felt my foot almost kick something.

It was too heavy and unnatural to be a rock or fallen branch so I moved my foot forward again and heard a 'thuck.'

I bent down and picked up something rectangular that had the weight of a small book. My camera! Excitement re-entered my body. Janine must have dropped it where those men couldn't find it. I pressed the round power button and a light flashed. Soon the 'Frame Ax' logo appeared on the screen. 'Bleep, bleep, bleep.' I quickly scrolled through some photos I took at home. Suddenly the photos turned black. *Useless night shots,* I thought. But wait. Could this be something? The zoom feature showed the photos Jinan had taken of trees, the clearing and some detailed shots of the men digging. Their faces were visible. *Wow,* I thought. *Thank goodness for the 'night vision' feature on my camera.* I stood where I was for a moment trying to organize my thoughts.

Okay, I told myself. *Jinan was right. Some seemingly important people were digging up things at night and it looked suspicious, but now what? Was the stuff even valuable and maybe they got permission from someone else to dig it? I had to collect everything I could about this... this... Mystery? Secret? I don't even know what to call it! Whatever.*

I ran through the forest knowing each step of the way that you would have thought it were the middle of the day. I crossed the river as I had several times before and soon found myself beneath the mini ravine. Jinan's cabin was straight ahead. I opened the door and with the help of my flashlight located the table that had the plates and spoons she had shown me not too long ago. I shoved them in my backpack right up against the clipboard that held my notes I had taken about everything I had seen that night. I dashed back in the direction I had come and managed to make it through the trees and bushes. Soon, I could see the tunnel where the raccoons and I had a showdown earlier that night. They were gone and I was able to get to the other side of the tunnel without anything blocking my path. I emerged from the oversized cylinder and was never happier to see my bike. I pushed it up the hill to the main street and pedalled home.

I left my bike at the side of the house and slipped in quietly through the back. I tiptoed up the stairs and opened my bedroom door. *Yes! I made it without...*

"Dhanika? You okay?" Dad was awake! I heard him get up and walk towards his door.

Oh, man. This is bad! What do I tell him?

"Yeah, I'm fine," I answered.

His door opened. "What are you doing up at this hour?" he asked sleepily. "And you still have your clothes on!"

"I fell asleep in them," I said.

Dad raised an eyebrow with suspicion and kept going. "Why were you coming up the stairs?"

"Just had to use the washroom."

"But there's one beside your room," he said.

"I know. I couldn't sleep so I went downstairs for a while," I lied. What else could I tell him? 'Dad, I was just at Sterling Creek Forest in the dead of night watching men dig up treasure and a woman was taking pictures of them?' That's crazy talk!

He shook his head in defeat. "Something else is going on," he said, almost to himself. "We'll talk about it tomorrow. Go back to bed."

"Okay. Good night," I replied, practically slamming my door shut.

I couldn't remember the last time I had such a restless sleep. I kept waking up every hour or two from strange and sometimes frightening dreams. One dream was men digging in a tunnel wearing raccoon suits. Another dream was of me trying to get through a dark, twisted maze with people chasing me. They had sharp, vampire teeth and kept snapping at my legs. The worst part was the noise they made as they got closer. Their screaming and crying filled my ears and got louder as they tried to grab and bite me. I pedalled faster but seemed to be sinking in the ground. My bike chain came loose and when I reached down to try and put it in place, I felt something warm and wet. I looked at my hands to see how much grease was on them and jumped back. It wasn't grease. My hands were covered in blood.

I woke up with a start and managed not to scream out loud. I looked around. My bedroom was untouched and sunlight began making its way through parts of my curtains. I peeked at my hands. My palms remained light brown with the same fortune teller lines running through them. My breathing slowed down and I shut my eyes. But wait! Wasn't I late for school? I sat up and could hear dad in his room. *No, you twit! It's Saturday!*

I went out to the side of the house and took a look at my bike. It wasn't as bad as I thought it would have been. It had thin patches of dirt on the frame and the tires were muddy but other than that it was okay. I put it in the garage and headed back inside.

The kitchen glowed with the bright rays of the June sun. I sipped a small glass of juice wondering what to do next. I had some evidence about what was happening in the forest but was it enough? What should I do with it now? And most importantly, what had happened to Jinan? Would I ever see her again? Where would I even begin to look?

There are things children know that grown-ups don't. We know where the best hiding spots are for hide and seek. We know where and when to do the perfect brussels sprout drops so our parents have no idea what's going on. Children can figure out video games and memorize song lyrics and playground chants without even having to write anything down. There comes a time when you have to forget about all of the stuff we can do that adults can't and work with them when a problem is so big you just don't know where to begin. This was one of those times. I had to use the help of an adult whom I could trust and had always been there for me as far back as I could remember. This person was going to be the one who...

"Morning Dhanika. Did you just open the garage door?"

Oh boy, I thought. *Here we go.*

"Dad, there's something I have to tell you."

Chapter 17

Some Guidance

Dad rested his hand on his chin and stared straight ahead. The low rumbling of the refrigerator was the only sound in the kitchen. We sat on opposite sides of the table. Between us on a frayed towel lay the objects from my backpack and a creased sheet with my charts and notes. I cleared my throat trying to disrupt the silence. He shook his head for the third time that morning, then spoke.

"Dhanika, what you've been doing has been irresponsible and dishonest. Not to mention dangerous! You could've been seriously hurt or killed all those times you went into that forest! Why did you keep doing that when there's a 'No Trespassing' sign on the forest fence and most importantly, why didn't you tell me this sooner?" I could see a little vein on the side of his head trying to nudge its way out.

This was worse than being questioned by Mr. Stellick and Mrs. Sharma. I was able to make stuff up that time they called me back to homeroom but dad knew me better than the two of them put together.

"I don't know," I said. "I thought Linh and I could handle it ourselves."

"You're just kids!" he exclaimed, raising his voice. "How long did you think you were going to be able to go there and keep it from me?"

I shrugged. "I kind of thought you were going to take their side. Like a grown-up versus kids thing."

"Dhanika, I don't agree with the idea of keeping children out of the forest," he said. "But rules need to be followed, even if you disagree with them!"

He ran three fingers across his mouth, closed his eyes, then opened them.

"Is Linh okay? I'm going to call her mom and dad to let them know what the two of you were..."

"Dad, no!" I interrupted. "She had nothing to do with it!" I was still hurt and angry that she thought I wasn't being a good friend but I knew that she was against the idea of entering Sterling Creek from the beginning. Even though we weren't speaking, I wasn't about to drag her down with me.

"What are you talking about?" he shot back. "Didn't you just say Linh knew about this?"

"Yeah," I replied. "But she tried to stop me from going into the forest the first time it happened." I removed a strand of hair from my face. "She hasn't been back since."

Dad's eyes moved left and right scanning the kitchen walls for answers. "Joss should have been here," he said, almost to himself and then cleared his throat. "To look out for you and make sure you're safe when I can't be here. Maybe I can get her to come in more during the week and on weekends."

"Dad, I'm not going to take off at night again and go back to the forest," I assured him. "I already told you I went after a rabbit I was trying to help. And if I hadn't come across Jinan, I probably wouldn't have gone back there ever!"

He got up, went to the fridge and returned with a can of Fruity Fizz. It hissed and cracked when he pulled the tab. He took a long sip and wiped his mouth.

I tried to make him less angry by pointing at the table. "And don't forget all this stuff. This is more serious than a couple of kids going into a forest."

Dad shook his head. "You're going to need more than what you've got here," he reminded me.

I stood up and raised my index finger to the air. "I do," I said. I ran up to my room and returned with my flashlight and camera. They'd been buried under a shirt and book I had in my backpack. Sliding the slim rectangular prism in front of him, I asked him to take a look at the pictures.

He scrolled through. "What's this? These are all black."

"Keep going," I said. "You'll see something."

Suddenly, dad almost dropped the camera. "Dhanika?" he asked quietly, picking it up again. "Is this...? I've seen these people before. They work for the city and in other public places, don't they?"

"Yeah, I think so," I replied.

"Oh my... this is really serious. I had no idea..."

"Neither did I."

He placed the camera down on the table and finished the rest of his drink. "Normally, I would have grounded you for a week because of all the sneaking out and dishonesty but Dhanika, you've definitely got something here."

I felt so proud at that moment even though I had been scolded just a few minutes earlier. It was as though I had been the first one to finish all of the math questions on a sheet and received a shiny sticker at the top of my page.

Excellent!

20 out of 20!

I tried to keep my cool because there was still work to finish. Dad got up and sat in the chair next to me.

"As dangerous and irresponsible as you acted, you've come up with some important evidence," he said, putting a hand on my forearm. He went on.

"But we can't just go after powerful men like the police chief and mayor ourselves. We have to be smart about it.

People like them don't solve problems on their own. They get lawyers in expensive suits to help them get what they want. So we need to do the same." He banged his fist on the table to show he meant business.

"How?" I asked.

"Leave it to me," he replied. "And Dhanika, from this moment on you've got to follow my instructions and do what I say. Any little mistake, whether you meant to do it or not, can make what you collected from the forest useless. Promise me you'll do exactly as I say."

Let's try this again, I thought. *This time's going to be different. No more sneaky business! Can I do this?*

I held out my right pinky and dad held out his. We interlocked and looked right at each other with sincerity and determination.

"Pinky promise," we said at the same time.

Dad got to work immediately by contacting a friend of his. He told me they went to university together. I saw and heard him speaking in low tones with the phone pressed to his ear that afternoon. Sometimes, he would raise his voice as if trying to get his point across but the person on the other end seemed to be doing more listening because there was barely a pause during the entire time dad spoke.

I felt relieved that I was no longer keeping secrets from him and had promised him that I wouldn't sneak out of the house, especially when it was dark and dangerous. We also agreed that I would tell no one of the things that I had seen and collected in the forest. These items were kept in a small locked trunk in the basement until we needed them again.

Jinan was right. What had been going on was bigger than a sign on the fence warning children to keep out. I missed her and wondered where she was but felt a warm closeness to my dad. The promise between him and me was like a second chance. I felt happy knowing that he was already beginning to trust me again. I also realized that it was careless of me to go biking off into the night into Sterling Creek Forest but assured him that I wouldn't do it again.

Our promise also got me thinking about other things that night when I lay in bed trying to read something for school. What had been happening at Spring Meadow over the last few days still bothered me. There was still a major problem that needed to be solved and talking about it with students and teachers would do nothing. I had to address this problem and was almost out of ways to solve it.

I took out my pen and notepad and began writing. I paused and looked through my window at the night sky.

What am I going to do?

I have no idea.

Chapter 18

Never Lose Your Flavour

It turns out I had been right. Dad's friend on the phone last week turned out to be a lawyer named Declan Morris. I wondered how they could have been friends in university and ended up working at different jobs. Dad explained that some of their classes were the same but something called their 'fields of study' was different. I never heard of a field of study and imagined it was a wide stretch of tall, leafy plants or fields of wheat where there were lots of books and people sitting and studying quietly.

Mr. Morris met with dad and me on Sunday. He and dad entered the kitchen and dad introduced us.

"Nice to meet you, Bhanika," he said, shaking my hand.

"It's Dhanika," I corrected.

"Dhanika," he repeated. "Sorry about that."

For the next hour or so, Mr. Morris listened as I spoke. He carefully wrote everything I told him about Sterling Creek Forest. Occasionally, he looked around the room as if he were putting pieces of a puzzle together in his mind. Once in a while dad would say something but I did most of the talking. I noticed he asked very specific questions and forced me to think back to the times I had visited Sterling Creek Forest.

"What did the police officer tell you when she saw you

going past the fence?"

"Uh... 'If you keep going, you'll lose the bike and... your life?'" I couldn't really remember. "Oh, no, no... 'You'll die!' I think that's it."

"Take your time but I need to know exactly what she said," he told me. "This is important. You said earlier that the officers were mean with their words. Not only is that something called a 'threat' and 'verbal abuse,' it's against the law for everyone including them to do!"

It was such a wonderful feeling knowing that not all adults stuck together to try to get children in trouble. I was happy to have two grown-ups in front of me who were on my side. I think that helped me open up quite a bit.

"I never thought the police could break rules," I said. "They're always telling us about safety and obeying traffic lights, signs and stuff."

"They're not all bad people," dad said. "But sometimes workers in all sorts of jobs can do bad things. That's how some people are."

Mr. Morris returned to his question. "Which one was it?" he asked. "What did the officer say?"

I thought back to that rainy evening and heard the officer's words in my head. I remembered how much they stung and hurt but now they seemed to have planted a tiny seed of anger inside me.

"'Keep going and you'll lose the bike and your life,'" I recalled. "Those were her words. She was the meanest cop I ever met."

His pen made short scratching sounds as it scraped against the white lined-paper. Finally, he clicked the pen shut and looked at me.

"I need to go over a bunch of things at my office tomorrow, but what you've uncovered out there is huge," Mr. Morris said stretching both arms out.

He continued. "For now, let's keep everything we discussed among the three of us. I'm going to present this to my partners where I work and get their ideas. Mr. Morris looked at me then dad. "I'll make sure this evidence is kept in a safe place."

"Thanks," dad replied.

"Good," Mr. Morris said. "I'll let you know when it has to be turned over to the police."

I thought for a moment. "What about Jinan?" I asked. "Can you find out what they did to her?"

"My guess is they put her in jail but I'll find out..."

"Jail?" I cried. "They can't do that to her! She needs to be at home with the flowers and trees and her cabin. That's not right!"

"What is and what's right are not always the same thing," Mr. Morris reminded me. "I'll find out for sure and make sure she's not being mistreated."

He stood up to leave. "Remember to keep everything a secret for now. Can you do that?"

I was about to reply but was interrupted.

"She can," dad answered, flashing me a quick wink.

***

The school hallways seemed to have an energy boost during the second last week of school. Students moved around quickly but dragged their feet to their next class. They seemed more interested in taking group pictures and spending more time at their lockers or outside on benches under shady trees. Groups of friends hung on to each other's shoulders and sometimes, without warning, threw their arms around each other. The Grade 8 students knew their time together was coming to an end, despite the promises they made to meet over the summer. Everything would be different in the fall—

new schools and teachers, locker combinations that had to be memorized and bigger hallways and classrooms to get used to.

I felt a bit sad and happy all at once. I was looking forward to the summer break with the hope that dad and I could go somewhere, even if it were just for a few days or a week or two. I always wanted to see different parts of the world.

I had not been at Spring Meadow long enough to feel attached to the place but was going to miss seeing the students in my classes. You don't realize how much time you spend with your classmates. The talks, jokes and more serious moments are things you miss when you have to leave them for the summer. I remember those feelings from my old school a year ago.

The last issue of the Monthly was printed early on Thursday morning. I stood by my locker looking for the article I wrote. It definitely wasn't as exciting as last month's front page news because it ended up on page five. I would have loved to have written or told someone about Jinan and the buried treasure in the forest but I had made a promise to dad and Mr. Morris not to say anything. I missed Jinan. This time, along with a bunch of other ones, was when I needed her the most. I wondered how she was doing in a cold, lonely jail cell away from the flowers, trees and water. I longed for her soft voice and beautiful singing and wondered if I would ever get to speak to her again.

Almost everyone at school was anticipating my article to go into more detail about the forest and the mysterious girl named 'R.' Students begged me to tell them about her, but I told them nothing. As I smoothed the paper out and read what I wrote, I smiled a bit, even though things weren't going very well. People who saw me doing this must have thought I was crazy but I didn't care.

WHY I AM A BAD FRIEND

Many students were expecting an update on what I wrote last month about the girl who went into Sterling Creek Forest and the big secret but this is more important.

A lot of autograph books and memory albums have been signed this month. We like to write things like 'Your friend' or 'BFF' just before we sign our names but what is a friend, really?

When you become popular, you get lots of attention. People you didn't speak to before come up to you and say nice things. They even want to be your friend. I think these people are like Colour Zaps. You know those cheap gumballs that come in packs of five? They're sweet in the beginning but after a minute of chewing, taste like paper. It took me a while to learn this, but now I realize what a bad friend I have been to two people. I won't use their names but they know who they are. Writing or saying sorry isn't enough, so here's what I think:

I am a bad friend because I ignored two girls who were very nice to me. They didn't care what clothes I wore, whether or not I have a cellphone or how many other friends I have. True friends laugh with you no matter how silly your jokes are or whatever kind of fool you make of yourself. Nice friends invite you for sleepovers and play all sorts of games, even if they're a bit babyish. You help each other in math class and eat freezies and D.D.Cs on hot days with them.

Whether you are back at Spring Meadow in September or moving to a new school, always be the best good friend you can be. Don't be a cheap gumball. No matter how sticky things get, never lose your flavour with true friends.

Have a great summer Spring Meadow!

Written by Dhanika Adhikari (Grade 7)

I folded the Monthly, tucked it between my legs and spun the dial on my lock a few times. The locker sprung open and I began removing a book and a few sheets of paper from my shelf.

"Hey," a voice said.

I looked up and saw Linh.

"Hi," I said.

We both looked around uncomfortably. Linh bent down and opened her backpack. She rummaged through it and took out her binder and pencil case. Then she straightened and said, "That was really nice what you wrote."

Joy and sadness were fighting each other inside me. I looked at her. "I'm really sorry about..."

"No, no," she interrupted, holding up her hand. "I'm sorry too. I was kind of mean to you."

"That's okay," I replied. "I shouldn't have hung out with those Grade 8 girls that day."

Linh pulled out some pencils, rulers and a wrinkled gym shirt and shoved them in her backpack. "Don't worry," she assured me. "I shouldn't control who you're friends with. You don't always have to be with me. It's not like we're married or anything!"

We both laughed.

"Hey, you doing anything after school?" she asked.

"No."

She smiled. "Want to get a D.D.C. together?"

"Sure!"

I shut the locker and we walked down the hallway to our next class.

Chapter 19

No Vacancy

The school year came to an end with the usual stuff. Locker cleanouts, whole school assemblies, movies and small parties in class took up the last two weeks of June. Sarah ended up reading the article I wrote in the Monthly and she and I had a short talk and exchanged apologies. Happy isn't even the word I should use to describe how I felt to have my closest two friends back. The three of us promised to meet in the summer and I even offered my house for a sleepover. We were giggly and excited about that.

With the help of the evidence Jinan and I collected, Declan Morris was able to get one of the lawyers from his firm to handle the case against the people who worked for the city as well as others who worked for the Sterling Creek Heritage Department. These six men also ratted out the managers of three businesses who were in on the illegal digging and cover-up. They were all charged with "failure to report artifacts and valuable items" and "using their positions of authority and public trust to conceal illegal activities." I thought there should have been another charge towards them; something that had to do with lying to the children of Sterling Creek in order to keep them from playing in the forest but Mr. Morris told me not to worry about it. The charges the group was facing were greater than lying to children. He, dad and I were on our way for a "special surprise" as Mr. Morris called it and were packed into his small car the very first day of the summer break.

"I know you feel cheated out of being kept out of Sterling Creek Forest all these years, Bhanika..."

"Dhanika," I corrected from the back seat.

"Yes!" he exclaimed, slapping a palm into his fist. He returned both hands to the steering wheel. "Why do I keep messing that up?"

I shrugged.

"Yes, well," he continued. "Those charges the men face are very serious. If found guilty, they're going to be fined and imprisoned."

"Wow," was all I could say.

Mr. Morris continued: "None of them is working at their regular jobs right now. They're at home waiting for the trial to begin. Kind of like being suspended from school."

"What's a trial?" I asked.

Dad took over. "It's a special meeting in a place called a courtroom where two sides or groups of people get to say their side of the story."

"There are also a judge and jury in the courtroom. The judge controls what's happening and what can be said and the jury is a group of citizens who listens to both sides and then decides who they think is guilty or not guilty," Mr. Morris said.

"When does the trial start?" I asked.

"Not for a while," replied Mr. Morris. "This one will start next year at the end of January."

"Next year? Why does it take so long?"

"Different reasons," he replied. "Evidence has to be verified, witnesses have to be named and arguments have to be prepared. Plus, there are so many other trials going on that have to get their turn in the courtroom."

We turned into the Frontier Motel. A blue 'No Vacancy'

sign flashed in front. There were about half a dozen cars in between the faded yellow lines of the parking lot. Mr. Morris reversed crookedly into one close to Room 108.

"What are we doing here?" I nervously asked.

"Someone asked to see you," dad answered.

The door slowly opened and a head emerged. I recognized the face right away. Jinan!

I pushed open the car door so hard I almost dented the jeep parked beside us. Jinan stepped out and I threw my arms around her. She bent slightly and hugged and patted my back. It was almost as though I had known her my whole life and she had just returned from a long trip. I finally let go and took a good look at her. Her face seemed cleaner and clearer and she was wearing new clothes.

"I missed you so much!" I said.

"I missed you too, Dhanika," she replied. She led me over to a couple of plastic white chairs and we sat down.

"I thought you were in jail," I told her.

"I was for a while," she said.

I leaned closer. "I've been dying to know what happened to you that night we were in the forest and those guys took you away."

"Well, I can't say too much," Jinan said. "Lawyer's instructions." She put her thumb and index finger together and ran it across her lips. "But I'm allowed to tell you that I was taken to an abandoned farmhouse just outside of Sterling Creek by those men you saw in the forest that night. They kept asking me for my camera and they searched me. It's a good thing you picked it up because they went back to that same spot the night after and tried to find it."

"Did the men hurt you?" I asked.

"No. The only painful parts were when they grabbed me from my hiding spot and dragged me across the clearing..."

"Yeah, I saw that! Sorry I couldn't help you."

"But you did help me. A lot. If you hadn't turned over everything you found to your dad and Mr. Morris, something even worse may have happened," Jinan said. She shuddered. "I don't even want to think what they would've done to me in that farmhouse if they kept me there for another day or two. I don't even know how to thank you."

"You don't have to," I said. "You're one of the nicest people I know."

She put her soft hand on my forearm. Right away I remembered how much I loved that feeling the first time she ever did that. I closed my eyes and enjoyed the moment. And to think I thought she was some evil witch who lived in a ratty cabin in the forest. It goes to show you things aren't always what they seem. We both looked around and were quiet for a short while. There was a hum as cars and trucks drove by. A couple of dogs barked somewhere. A cool breeze settled in and the sun shyly moved behind some shifting, greyish clouds but didn't disappear entirely. It was almost as if Jinan were making the summer heat a little more comfortable.

I pointed my thumb backwards towards her door. "Is this your new home?" I asked.

"For now," she said. "Until they let me go. Then I'll return to the forest when they're not looking." She smiled mischievously.

I thought for a moment. "Maybe you could live with us. Yeah! That's a good idea. We have an extra room and you could meet Linh and Sarah. I think you'd really like..."

Jinan held up her hand. "That's so kind of you, Dhanika. But I belong among the trees. Remember when I told you about all of that?"

My excitement evaporated. "Yes. It's just that I like you and want to be friends with you for a long time even if you're a grown-up."

She laughed. "Dhanika, no matter where I end up I will

never forget you. You were so helpful and never betrayed me. I will always be grateful. But live your life the way you have been all this time. Be a kid." She paused. "I mean a child. You're not..."

"A baby goat," I finished. We both laughed.

Jinan continued. "Play with your friends, go to the movies and ride your bike." She paused then smiled. "Just don't be wasteful and take more than you need or I'll come back and get mad at you. Or haunt you!" She made a cute, spooky face.

I laughed and nodded. "I promise. Will you be okay?"

"Sure. You know how much I love the forest. I'll be fine." Jinan looked toward dad and Mr. Morris. "I think you should go now. They've been waiting."

I gave her a long hug knowing she wasn't my mom but in that short moment I pretended she was.

"I'll miss you," I told her. "Can I come back to visit?"

"Of course," she replied. "You know where to find me."

I turned my head and watched Jinan wave as the car pulled out of the motel parking lot. A common pattern I noticed over the past few months was how happiness and sadness could occur at the same time. I was elated to see Jinan but it really hurt to let go. Sometimes the hardest, most difficult things we have to do are also the ones that are necessary.

Later that evening, unbeknownst to me, something happened at that motel. Its sign had changed. It continued to flash but now the blue word was 'Vacancy.'

Chapter 20

Food Court Closure

I thought the excitement would go away after Mr. Morris's lawyer friend presented the evidence Jinan and I had collected to the police. Nothing could be further from that. Newspaper and magazine reporters from across the province wanted to speak to me. People from radio and TV programs wanted interviews too.

Our front door had been knocked on so many times I was afraid it was dented. The doorbell switch was being pushed more than it had ever been since we moved into the house. At first, I felt the way I did when *The Monthly* printed my article about Sterling Creek Forest. After a while, though, it started bugging me quite a bit. Every time I tried to settle down to read, watch something on TV or meet Linh or Sarah, somebody was in the doorway who wanted "a quick word."

The reporters were friendly, well-dressed grown-ups who spoke smoothly, smelled nice and smiled probably more than they needed to. They did a good job explaining everything they and their group were going to do. Their group was usually a camera operator and someone controlling the lights or someone with a makeup case.

I wondered what the students at *The Monthly* would think if I told them I got to meet actual reporters. After the explanations, they got down to work and boy, were the questions endless!

"What made you decide to explore the forest?"

"Can you describe what you saw?"

"How did you feel when you were in there?"

"What made you decide to go back?"

"Who was the woman in the forest?"

"Dhanika, in your own words, can you tell me what happened when you saw the artifacts being dug up that night?"

What a strange question, I thought. *'In my own words? Who else's words could they be?'*

After the fifth or sixth reporter left, dad had had enough.

"That's it!" he announced, shutting the door behind a group from a big radio station in the city. "We can't go on... you shouldn't have to put up with all those questions!"

"It's okay, dad," I said. "They're not hard to answer and a lot of them are the same questions."

"That's not the point," he replied, kicking some shoes into the closet and sliding the door shut. "Those reporters should respect our privacy. You and I are going to come up with a schedule."

"What kind of schedule?" I asked.

"One that shows the times you're available to talk," he replied. "I don't want strangers coming in and out of our house the way they have been over the last few days." He went upstairs, returned with his laptop and began typing away.

"What are you writing?" I asked.

"Actually, I was just about to ask you. What times would you like to meet with the reporters? I don't want them bothering you when you want to go out and play or help me make chicken wings or cookies!"

I smiled and moved closer to dad on the couch. I leaned my head on his shoulder as he put together a chart that we would later print and tape on our front door. Dad had come up with a good idea but it left me unsure as to whether or not it would be followed.

The next morning, dad and I were sitting in the kitchen. In front of us were some slices of toast and two tall, fruit smoothies. He uses a special blend of blueberries, strawberries, bananas and milk. Sometimes he adds pomegranate juice of which he warns me to be careful. "If any of that stuff gets on your clothes be prepared to have it on you for a long time!"

I sipped the thick liquid and sat back. The bright sunlight shone through the window and spilled yellow on the floor like a huge spotlight. The birds on a nearby branch chirped merrily. Everything seemed perfectly in place. I began eating the warm bread, wiping a few crumbs from the side of my mouth.

Dad's cellphone buzzed. He picked it up, said a few short words, sighed and placed it back on the table.

"What happened?" I asked.

"Nothing serious. I just need to go in to work for an hour." He paused. "You want to come in with me or are you going to be okay here?"

"Actually, I was planning to meet Linh later on this morning," I told him. "At her house."

Dad stood up. "Good. I'll be back before one. Don't stay outside too long. It's going to get really hot."

"I won't."

He was about to head upstairs when the doorbell rang.

"Those reporters!" he cried. "Can't they read a piece of paper that's right in front of them?" He stomped towards the door and flung it open. "She'll be ready to talk at 2. That's what the schedule's for!"

As I sat at the table, I could hear a woman's voice. Dad seemed to calm down quickly because I could barely hear anything he was saying. I wondered why she still hadn't left. The two of them seemed to be at our front entrance for a long time. I got up to see what was taking so long. Dad met me halfway. His face looked blank as though he'd forgotten how to speak.

"Dhanny," he began. "You don't have to... I mean, you may not be ready..."

"Ready for what?" I asked. "Does the reporter want to meet with me now? How many people are with her?"

Dad knelt down until we were at eye level.

"That's no reporter." He gently pulled me closer.

"It's your mother."

***

It was the slowest, most difficult walk I'd ever done. Even going up to that cabin or walking through the forest at night felt easier than this. My legs were weighed down and getting pulled towards the floor as I took short heavy steps. *Was I walking on something sticky?* I looked down. No, the floor looked fine. I stopped at the doorway and stared at the woman dressed in a light blue, sleeveless shirt and beige pants.

Her skin was a smooth brown with a few sharp lines coming out from the sides of her dark eyes. I thought her lips could have been less shiny red and planned to squirm away if she tried to kiss me. She had straight brown hair that was combed back and held together at the top in a pony-tail. A strand of it swung near the right side of her face. I remember dad telling me how much we looked alike. I looked closely at her features as though she were some zoo animal but didn't see any resemblance.

She swung her white purse back and bent slightly. "Hello, Dhanika," she said.

I don't know what it was about her voice. Maybe I began remembering times she spoke to me when I was really young or maybe it was the warmth it carried but I fell into a trance. This voice, from a long time ago, had returned and took control of how I felt. But I had to make sure it was her this time.

"H... Hi."

She smiled and once again the combination of curved lips and almost perfect teeth made me lose my senses. For a minute, I didn't believe this was actually happening right in front of me.

"How've you been?" she asked.

"O... Okay. D... Do you... Are you... Do you live in the forest?" I managed to ask.

Her laugh reminded me of Jinan's.

"No, no! It's a long story and there's so much I need to tell you. Can we go somewhere and talk?" She opened up her purse and removed a set of keys.

I looked over to dad, who nodded.

Turning back to her, I said, "Okay." I then opened the closet door and pulled out my shoes.

***

Brookville Mall was packed. I should have known it would be this way seeing how it's the first week of the summer vacation. Luckily, mom and I managed to find two seats in the busy food court. She shook a sugar packet before ripping it open allowing it to snow down on her dark coffee. I sipped a medium lemonade while waiting for my small container of fries to cool down.

"Dhanika, it's so nice to see you," she said.

I nodded. What was I supposed to say now? 'Yeah, you too?' The truth is, I didn't know what to feel. This woman had been gone for so many years and she just came out of nowhere acting as if nothing happened. I looked around at the nearby fountain and teenagers who were walking nearby talking and loudly joking around.

She continued. "I know this is hard for you but I want to try and make things easier for you from now on. I was thinking of being around more often..."

Suddenly, I wanted answers. I needed to understand. This person left me and I wanted to know why.

"Why are you here?" I asked sharply. It was as if being in the forest all those times gave me a superpower or at least a boost of courage. Mom seemed a bit surprised.

"I came to see you," she replied.

"No. I mean, why'd you come back now?"

Mom tapped her stir stick against the table and then bent it from side to side. "The truth is, I heard about the mystery you solved in a news magazine and was amazed, excited and proud... So many things were going through my mind when I read what you did that I just had to..."

"So that's why you came back? Because I got a little famous?" I demanded. Feelings of hurt and anger stung my sides.

She put her hand up as though I'd just thrown something at her. "No, no. I didn't mean it that way. The publicity you got was that... thing... sort of the final push I needed to see you. Believe me, Dhanika, it hasn't been easy being away from you all these years."

The fries were a bit cooler. I picked up three and ran them through some ketchup before placing them in my mouth. Mom handed me a napkin when she saw I was about to use the back of my hand.

"Where have you been?" I asked.

Mom took another sip of coffee. I thought the gloss and lipstick and who-knows-what-else was going to come off but her lips remained shiny.

"All over the place," she said. "Nassau, Vancouver, Atlanta... Mostly Nassau."

"Why?"

"Work stuff," she replied. "Setting up different regional programs, meetings and desk work. Grown up stuff."

"Dad's a grown up and he's around to help take care of

me," I reminded her. "Why couldn't you do that too?"

Mom sighed. "Dhanika, it's not that easy. Moms and dads love their children but it's not always easy for them to love each other. Sometimes they can't live with each other and have to move away."

Anger pricked me again. "But you just left me! No calls, e-mails, nothing!" My voice grew louder. "What about all those times when I needed to talk to you? To hug you? Do you know what it's like to see other people with their moms and I don't have one!?" I banged my hand on the table. A few drops of lemonade escaped the cup.

She leaned closer to me. I wanted to push her face, wet lips and all, out of the way but managed to keep my cool.

"You don't think I missed you? Do you think I didn't care?" Mom wiped her eyes with a napkin. "It was harder on me than you realize!"

I softened a bit and was quiet. I have a weakness when I see people close to crying or in any kind of pain.

She continued. "Adults aren't perfect and don't have all the answers. You'll learn as you get older, things aren't always what they seem." She began playing with the stir stick again. This time she bent it too much and it broke. "Just because I wasn't around and didn't keep in touch doesn't mean I don't love you. Well, I'm telling you now, it was hard for me to call or e-mail you all those years," she explained. "I knew how well you got along with your dad and just left it at that. I knew you were in good care. Do you understand what I'm saying?"

"No," I said flatly.

Mom tried again. "It's like exercising, cooking or learning a craft," she explained. "You know how to do it but after a while not practising, you forget. You have to try and re-learn it. That's what I'm trying to do with you."

I didn't even want to look at her so I turned to the side and faced some plants.

"Dhanika, believe me. I want to make things better. You don't know how sorry I am for being away all this time. Can you find it in you to forgive your mother?" She sat back in her seat as though she'd just run a marathon.

I wanted to cover my ears but something about the way she spoke made me feel as if she meant what she was saying. I played with a few hovering leaves, remembering two weeks ago when Linh and I said sorry at our locker. Was it my turn to be the forgiver now?

"Is it still on you?" I asked her.

"What?" mom asked with a confused look.

I showed it to her. Without hesitating, she reached down the neck of her shirt and pulled out the pendant.

I raised an eyebrow. "You still have it," I said with barely any expression.

She nodded. "It always made me feel close to you."

"Close to me?" I repeated. "Okay. But how special is this really? Didn't you get it from some store?"

Mom leaned in close again. "Yes. But where did my macaroni necklace come from?"

"I made it for you when I was in Grade 1."

She nodded. "And what about the watch made out of shiny, plastic beads?"

"That was when I was in Grade 2."

"But didn't the other kids make those for their moms?"

"Yeah."

"Were those any more or less important than the one you made?"

I shook my head. "All of them were special."

"You see," she told me. "It doesn't matter where these objects come from. The important thing is what they mean between the two people who give and receive them."

She reminded me of Jinan when she touched my forearm. I gave her a hint of a smile.

"Dhanika, I'm not trying to tell you that everything will get back to normal. But some things will change. I plan to move back to Hammondville. I'll be starting a new job around there and will be able to see you a lot more. It doesn't mean your dad and I will live together." She paused and sipped her coffee. The face she made told me that it had gotten cold. "I promise to try and see you more than I have over the years. But I'm not going to force you to do anything. I'll be sad but will understand if you don't want to see me again."

I wasn't sure what to say. Maybe I gave her a nod or some other head movement.

"Think about it and let me know."

We stood up with our empty cups and looked around for garbage and recycling bins. As we made our way towards the food court exit, two young women in black skirts pounced and quickly slid into our empty seats as we walked out. You would never have known that one of the most serious mother-daughter talks had just taken place beside the leafy, artificial plants and at the table with drops of lemonade and coffee.

We walked past two young women using cellphones. Their pace was slowed by their bent necks. One of them spoke:

"Looks like Val's getting promoted."

"No way! She's like the worst manager ever!" the second one replied.

"Don't worry," the first one assured her friend. "I've got so much dirt on her. By the time I'm finished with her, the only job she'll have is mopping the floors of this food court!"

They both laughed. The first one continued.

"But don't tell anyone. This is just between you and me. It's our secret."

Seems like the woods aren't the only one watching.

Epilogue

The cool wind nudges the trees as they find a rhythm with their carefree swaying. They rest momentarily and then continue, this time in a sluggish waltz. Shimmering yellow and orange leaves seem to twinkle in the autumn sun. The sharp air is filled with the scent of distant, burning fires and a warning that colder, whiter days lie beyond the horizon.

A squirrel darts from behind some bushes, blinks and looks around. She quickly bolts to the left, making sharp turns and pounces on a chestnut. Clasping it in her paws, she holds it to her twitching nose and begins gnawing and rotating until only the top, bottom and centre remain. The squirrel runs off in search of some more food to put away in her hollowed-out abode at the base of an ancient oak tree. Just above, two robins chirp a forgotten tune from long ago before joining their southbound friends in the sky.

At first, the Sterling Creek Forest seems as it always was—thick, green and untouched. A closer look shows paved bike paths, black and brown steel lamp posts and wooden benches. Signs serve as reminders to pick up after pets and warnings about littering, vandalism and fires. The forest is now a place for plants, wildlife and people to get together and enjoy the shade, warmth and everything else that makes it a special place of natural beauty. Children ride on its paths. Mothers push strollers among the trees laughing with other parents whose children tug at their hands, trying to break free and explore this wonderful and exciting space. Grown-ups of different ages sit on benches talking about life and a time when the forest was a restricted place.

The people who made it that way were found guilty of theft and failing to report uncovered artifacts to the authorities. The surrounding fence and signs warning children to keep out were removed and work began right away to make the forest open to everyone.

Mom and dad never got back together but I got used to it. Mom lives in nearby Hammondville and dad moved into an apartment in downtown Sterling Creek. Joss also left and started a family of her own when I was around fifteen and old enough to be on my own at home. I see my mother more than before. We get together a couple of times a month to talk or have coffee or dinner. Sometimes I take different foods over or she tries to make things herself. She is still not much of a cook but I don't have the heart to tell her she's not as good as dad. Strange, isn't it? Aren't moms usually better than dads when it comes to cooking?

Linh, Sarah and I ended up going to the same high school but we each went to different universities. After a while, we made new friends and talked to each other less frequently. We communicate through texts and e-mails but are not as close as when we went to Spring Meadow. It's a sad fact of life. Friends drift apart even when you don't want it to happen. The important thing is to enjoy the time you spend together, the jokes, D.D.C, bike rides and talks for they don't last forever.

Sadly, the same thing happened with Jinan. Actually, it was worse. After the trial, Jinan disappeared from the motel where she was staying and I never saw her again. Sometimes when I'm walking through Sterling Creek Forest or any other wooded area, I look closely among the trees trying to detect any sign of her.

Jinan was one of those neat, interesting people who was so unique, she was almost magical. Everything about her—the way she moved, spoke and sang—made me think she was some kind of fairy of the trees assigned to protect the entire forest, yet one who ended up choosing me as her helper. I remember how scared I was when we first met.

There are also memories I have of her telling me about the secrets of the forest and how I, as ordinary and plain as I felt back then, was going to be the one to initiate change. I can remember her laugh, the way she touched my arm and ways she helped me when I was hurt. Jinan was like a mother to me, who came at the right time when my real mom was not around. I take comfort knowing that she is probably bonding happily with nature wherever she is.

The older you get, the more often you reminisce using words like "I remember." But they're not just words older people use. Even as we go through elementary school, as children, we're always thinking about and talking to our friends about what we miss about Grade 3, the games we played in class and how Ms. Simmonds was "the best Grade 1 teacher in the world."

I guess we all grow up quickly. One moment you're a girl who has moved to a new school and is nervously looking around her Grade 7 class one morning and before you know it, she's taller, with a different voice and new responsibilities.

So who is this girl now?

My name is Dhanika Yadav. I'm telling you this because my name is important and so am I.

I'm important not only because I am now 34 and the mother of a nine-month-old baby boy. It feels incredible knowing that I helped give Sterling Creek Forest back to the community. People who remember what happened sometimes see and thank me for standing up to those who stole from the forest and the community. Actions are what people remember the most.

I try to live these beliefs of mine every day. I work as a veterinarian at a clinic near my townhouse and have seen all kinds of issues with animals and the people who take care of them. My salary isn't great but I get this incredible, warm feeling when I leave the clinic at night, knowing that I did my best to help an injured or sick animal. It is indescribable. And just seeing the looks of happiness on pet owners' faces when I tell them that their dog or parrot is going to be fine, it is as though I have given them new life with my words.

I hear crying in the next room. My son has woken up. As a mother, I can always tell what he is feeling by the sound of his cry. This one tells me he feels scared and alone and needs someone to hold him and tell him he'll be okay.

I enter the room and lift him out of the crib and whisper softly to him. He cries a bit less and I know that my words aren't going to keep him this way for very long so I try something else. Holding him closer, I begin singing softly:

When the last ray of sun goes down
And the cold and dark are all around
Don't fear, cry or shake
Warm in my arms you'll be
When you awake.

His eyes close slowly and I gently place him back down. *I will keep him safe,* I think to myself. *I'll love and protect him as long as I'm alive, making sure he gets to see and feel the beautiful things this troubled world still has.*

Before closing the door quietly, I make sure the window is locked and the curtains are drawn tightly before I switch off the blue and yellow lamp on the dresser. A wave of black engulfs the room sending shivers of uncertainty throughout those who are in it. But beside the crib, a small nightlight shines.

After all, you are never too young or old for a little help when it is dark.

THE END

Acknowledgements

The author would like to thank:

Sabi Jailall for editing and revising this book.

Cheryl Antao-Xavier for her help with revising and publishing this book.

Peter Jailall for his encouragement and guidance.

Robert McCallum for his opinions and suggestions.

Al and Ogi. Both of you were with this story from the very beginning when it was stapled photocopies in our small group meetings. I am grateful for and will never forget those fun sessions of sharing, encouragement and support.